# The Secret of the Seven Valleys

Dan DeKoning

Cover Design by GetCovers

ISBN: 978-1-963691-04-7

# DEDICATION

This book is dedicated to the Geocaching community.
To hiders, finders, and those behind the scenes.


See you on the trail!

# The Secret of the
# Seven Valleys

# CHAPTER ONE

The elevator bell dinged, the doors slid open, and Drake Decker exited the elevator carrying a cardboard box loaded with white paper bags filled with Chinese takeout food. He navigated the hallway until he at last reached room four hundred and stopped before the door. He attempted to hold the box in a way to allow him to dig the room key from his front pocket, but the bundle was too far off balance for that. Afraid to spill the box and too lazy to set it down on the floor, Drake kicked the door three times.

He waited a few seconds, and at last heard the chain slide away from the door and the security lock disengage. The door opened, and he saw the bright hazel eyes of his girlfriend.

"Sorry, wrong room. We didn't order anything,"

"Come on, let me in, Geneva. This box is getting heavy."

Geneva stepped aside and held the door for Drake. He entered the room and made a beeline for the only table at which two women were overlooking one laptop and taking notes. The blonde noticed his approach, gathered up the papers, and moved them and the computer to a nearby dresser.

Drake set the box on the table, and the three women began

extracting the bags from the box. Once it was empty, Drake dropped it on the floor.

The blonde opened a bag, extracted the white cubed container, and opened it. "Who ordered the noodles?"

The redhead half-raised her hand. "I did."

Ingrid passed the Lo Mein and a pair of chopsticks to Allie and selected another bag to open. It didn't take her long to distribute the remaining meals, and soon they all dove into dinner, chopsticks waving wildly, except for Drake, who took the less-traditional route and used a fork.

"This reminds me of Chinatown," Geneva said. "Every time Ingrid and I go to the theater, we stop either after or before the show in this little restaurant on Oxford Street. I love Chinese food."

"Did you gals get far in the planning?" Drake asked before selecting his next piece of honey chicken.

Allie sucked in a noodle, quickly chewed and swallowed. "We're getting there. I wish we'd done more research over the last few months."

"Are you getting stuck on anything I might help with?" Drake asked.

Ingrid shook her head. "Not really. Fortunately, where we're going, there aren't a ton of geocaches to select from. Maybe a hundred in all. We made a first pass and removed anything greater than a terrain rating of four since we don't want to do anything Allie would have trouble with because of her knee."

"My knee is fine," Allie said.

"Then why didn't you want to do that marathon with me?" Ingrid asked.

"Because I couldn't make it out here that weekend, remember? I had that other thing going on. The one I told you about," Allie tried to explain, generating the least lame excuse she could think of.

"I'm surprised she agreed to this trip," Drake said. "She is still wary about steep hills since she wrecked her knee a couple of years ago."

"Drake, I'm not wary. I simply don't bound up and down them like a mountain goat anymore. I like to take my time," Allie countered.

Ingrid shoved her chopsticks into the takeout container and placed it on the table. "Anyway, once we knocked out anything greater than terrain four, that narrowed it down to about fifty."

"That many?" Geneva asked.

Allie nodded. "Apparently, they like the geocaches challenging in the Alps. Now it's simply been a matter of translating the descriptions from Italian to English."

"Are there any puzzle caches?" Drake asked.

Allie grinned. "We're saving those for you since we realize you love figuring those out."

Drake groaned, and his lips formed into a pout. "Really?"

The three women laughed.

"Of course not. Geneva's been working on those," Allie said. "Maybe you would give her a hand after lunch."

Drake produced a grin that would make any sly fox proud. "Of course. I'd love to."

"She meant a hand with the puzzle," Allie clarified.

The women laughed again, and Drake joined in this time.

"We should have gone to Denmark instead," Ingrid said. "I would have translated for you, and we wouldn't have to do all this pre-work. And I could show you the village my parents are from."

"I don't know. I liked the way we came up with this idea. Everyone submitting three ideas, then picking one at random from a hat seemed the fairest way to select this year's geocaching trip," Geneva said.

Ingrid capitulated. "Okay. I suppose. You've got food on your chin, buddy."

Drake rose and ambled to the mirror. He took a close look

and spotted a smudge of orange sauce just below his chin that he wiped away with the back of his hand. He continued his inspection to make sure he was clean, and his hazel eyes drifted to his blond hair. Drake normally kept it in a tight, close cut, but since Geneva liked it longer, he was attempting to grow it out. Instinctively, he patted his belly. Normally, he liked to keep his average build at a hundred and ninety pounds, but he'd ballooned to three pounds heavier over the summer. Satisfied that he looked okay, he returned to the table.

"Did anyone learn how to explain geocaching in Italian?" Drake asked.

"I can barely explain it in English," Ingrid said.

"What do you tell people?" Drake asked.

"That I'm looking for things people have hidden."

"I always compare it to a high-tech scavenger hunt. That seems to help," Allie said. "I only get into the details if people seem interested, but usually that simple explanation works the best for me."

"So does anyone know how to say scavenger hunt in Italian?" Drake asked.

"I learned how to say I don't speak Italian," Geneva said.

Drake thought for a second, then shrugged. "That will work. Everyone done eating?"

No one said otherwise, so Drake and Allie cleared the mess from the table, and Drake gathered it all into the box.

"I'll take this to the garbage outside," he said.

"I got it," Allie offered. She took the box and left the room.

As soon as the door clicked shut, Drake turned to Ingrid. "You're not looking for anything higher than a terrain of three, right? Allie plays off that injury, but she's still having problems with that knee, even though that accident was two years ago."

"Of course. I set the filter at four, since that's what she said, but I've been ignoring every terrain rating more than a three. Most of the ones I've written down are lower than that. I don't enjoy the thought of seeing her in pain either, Drake."

Drake nodded. "Good. I wasn't happy about this location at first. I was hoping we'd pick something flatter, like Florida, but who could have guessed Allie herself would have submitted a challenging place?"

"Why did she do that?" Geneva asked.

"She's always trying to push herself, even though there's nothing for her to prove. So, that said, what do y'all need help with?"

"You could check the equipment. Make sure we're not forgetting anything," Geneva suggested. "While you're doing that, we'll continue with the list and solving any puzzle caches."

Drake nodded. On the dresser were four matching mini backpacks. He gathered them up and carried them to the bed. To get comfortable, he pulled his chair from the table and sat at the bed's edge. Although the backpacks were identical, he could tell who owned which one based on the pins they'd attached to the flap on the front. Allie had a Marine Corps emblem, based on her time in the service. Geneva's pin was a treble clef, which was apropos since she played cello in the symphony and often conducted. Ingrid was a bit more on the nose with a pin of the Danish flag, a field of red with a white Nordic cross. Drake when the obvious route with a geocaching pin and a compass.

Drake heard a knock at the door, and since he was closest, he got up from his seat, opened it, and found Allie standing there.

"I locked myself out," Allie explained.

Drake let her in and returned to the bags while Allie returned to the computer.

Drake opened his bag first and dumped all the contents onto the bed. As he picked items from the pile, he placed them in a neat row. In order, he lined up a handheld GPS, four extra batteries, tweezers, a compact mirror, a mini notebook, a half dozen gel pens with black ink, a small flashlight, a multi-tool, and a compass. He studied the pile for a moment.

"I feel like we're missing something here," he said, looking up from his stash. "Can someone else come take a look?"

Ingrid and Allie seemed focused on the laptop. "I got it," Geneva said. "I'm just looking over shoulders, anyway."

Geneva joined Drake and went through each of the items, pointing at each of the items as she called them out.

"Do you think this is everything?" Drake asked. "After all, it's been four months since we put this list together."

Geneva snapped her fingers, the pop loud enough to get Allie's attention. "You're missing the cache list and the maps. Hopefully Allie and Ingrid will finish the list soon, and we'll pick up the maps when we get to Italy."

Drake scanned the pile again. "I feel like we're not bringing enough."

Geneva shrugged. "This is what we all agreed to. Just the basics, so wouldn't have to haul too much with us."

"It kind of takes me back to when I first started," Drake said. "I'd go out looking for geocaches with only my Garmin and a pen. None of all the fancy things we carry today."

"I started out the same, but I have to admit, I don't know what I'd do without some of these things."

Geneva picked the mirror off the bed and opened it. "Do you know how many times I've almost blindly put my hand into a spider's web or a hornet's nest and this simple thing saved me from a nasty bite or worse? I also never go out geocaching anymore without a pair of tweezers in my pocket. So much better than trying to use a small stick to extract a stuck log from a container. Honestly, if it were just me, I'd just take these two things and leave the rest."

"Same," Drake said. "But Allie insisted we all have a multitool, a compass, and a flashlight with us."

"And you'll be glad you do if you get lost in the woods again," Allie said, peeking over the laptop.

Drake rolled his eyes. "It was only the one time. One!"

"Yeah. For six hours."

"I made it back eventually," Drake said in his own defense.

Geneva glanced at Allie and raised an eyebrow. "Is that true?"

Allie grinned. "That's his story to tell, not mine. Go ahead, Drake, you've got the floor."

Everyone's attention turned to Drake, and when he'd had enough of the uncomfortable silence, he broke it.

"Okay, so I wandered around for a while. I made it to a clearing, climbed over a fence, and found myself in a pasture. Then I found a kind farmer, and his wife gave me a ride to the trailhead."

"You left a couple things out there, Duck-man. Care to fill in the blanks, or shall I?" Allie said.

Drake's cheeks reddened. "Okay, okay. So, I climbed over the fence and made it halfway across the pasture when I spotted a bull with a full head of steam running toward me. Seeing that rampaging beast, I took off like a shot and ran as fast as I could toward the barn I'd spotted. I was about at the gate when I slipped on a fresh bull patty, spun around, and caught the butt of my jeans on the barbed wire fence. I heard someone call out and when I turned around to face the angry farmer who was in the middle of accusing me of stealing his prize bull, I ripped the seat from my jeans."

Geneva, while listening to the story, attempted to appear supportive, but couldn't hold her laughter anymore and it came gushing out. Ingrid and Allie joined in as well, and Drake didn't think it was funny at all.

Geneva wiped the tears from her eyes and stopped laughing long enough to press him to finish the story.

"Well, the farmer opened the gate for me, and walked me to the farmhouse with my torn jeans and my butt exposed to the world. He wanted to call the sheriff and have me arrested for trespassing, but lucky for me, his wife was a kind soul and offered to give me a ride off the property."

The women laughed again and kept at it until the titters finally died down.

"And that's why we'll carry the compass and the other stuff," Allie inserted.

"Yeah, yeah. I got you," Drake said as he shoved the items back into his bag.

After he returned the items to his bag, Drake grabbed the next one in line, which turned out to be Ingrid's. Besides the same items as were in his, she also carried hand sanitizer, lotion, lip balm, and eyeliner. He checked out Allie's bag next, and in hers he discovered a baseball cap and a Garmin for their rental car. Geneva's bag contained the same items as Drake, except she also had a small sandwich baggie filled with euros.

"What about other gear? Shouldn't we have packed for cold weather? Boots, gloves, that sort of thing?" Drake asked.

"No need," Geneva answered. "I checked the local weather for everywhere we intend on visiting in the next few days, and all the snow is gone for the year, and they expect the temperatures to be warm for our entire visit."

Drake shrugged. "Okay. If you say so, I'm not going to worry about it. Are you two finished with the plan yet?"

"Almost," Ingrid said. "Hold your horses."

"I can't. I'm too excited. You know I've never been to Italy before," Drake said.

"No big deal," Geneva said. "It's just like going to Pennsylvania, except the pasta is better."

"Pennsylvania?" Drake asked. "Really?"

Geneva winked at him, then gave him a kiss on the forehead. "You're so gullible. One of the many things I love about you."

"Here's what we have," Allie said. "Tomorrow, we fly to Milan, then pick up our rental and head to Como. The following morning, we can grab a couple of local caches in Como, then head up into the mountains for the good stuff."

"Why can't we start caching right away," Drake said. "Why waste an entire day?"

"Because we don't land in Milan until almost nine at night," Ingrid said. "And then there's the long drive. I'm sure we'll all be dead tired and ready for bed by the time we get to Como. If you really feel the need to find a geocache, there seems to be an easy one only three blocks from the hotel."

Drake leaned over and took Geneva's hand in his. "I'm really looking forward to taking this trip with you. I had hoped for something more romantic, like Paris or Rome, but I'm sure this will be a great experience for us."

"Come on, Drake, what could be more romantic than the two of us together in the beauty of the Italian Alps?"

Ingrid coughed to get their attention. "Other than your best friends along for the ride? Right Allie?"

Allie smiled. "Who's saying that those two aren't going to spoil our romantic vacation? I've always wanted to visit the Alps. I hope we'll have time to do some sightseeing too. Catch a few museums, or some art galleries?"

"I may have accidentally researched a few of those. Along with a romantic boat tour for two on Lake Como," Ingrid said.

"Don't you mean romantic boat tour for four?" Drake asked.

Ingrid smiled. "Sorry. From what I understand, it's a small boat."

Geneva laughed. "We'll just have to find a way to amuse ourselves while they're gone, Drake."

Drake kissed the back of Geneva's hand. "I think that's doable." His voice turned serious. "Have you thought about what we talked about? You moving to Nashville to be with me?"

"To be honest, I haven't had much of a chance to mull it over. I've been so busy with planning the new season of the symphony. It would be a tremendous change for me, Drake. Moving from Boston to Nashville. What would I do there? Does

Nashville even have a symphony?"

Drake shrugged. "We've got an Opry. That's pretty much the same."

"Drake Decker, that's nowhere near the same thing," Allie scolded. "And to answer your question, Geneva, Nashville, has an excellent symphony orchestra. To be honest, if you're considering his offer, you should come visit us for a while, see how you'd like the small-town vibes."

"Nashville is hardly a small town," Geneva said.

"True, but neither of us live right in the city. I'm about twenty minutes out. Drake's probably thirty-five, depending on traffic. I think you'd like it. There's a more laid-back way of life, plenty of places to park, and people don't lean on their car horns."

It was Ingrid's turn to get angry. "So, what, you two would take my best friend from me and leave me here all alone in this metropolis?"

"Of course not, dear. I've already cleared some space for you in my house," Allie said. "You can have the guest room. It has its own bathroom, an empty closet, and my granddaddy's dresser just waiting for your things."

Ingrid pouted again. "So, you'd just shove me in the guest room, like a common…guest?"

"No. I said I had plenty of room for your things in the guest room," Allie answered.

"This is getting much too sappy for my tastes," Drake said. "Perhaps we should save all the big life-changing decisions for after this trip. After all, I've heard that you don't really get to know a person until you've traveled internationally with them."

Geneva raised her eyebrow, not buying a word. "Is that even true?"

"I don't know. It could be. Either way, we should all get some rest. It's a long flight and a busy day tomorrow."

# CHAPTER TWO

By the time the group arrived at their small boutique hotel in Como, checked in, and found their rooms, the clock showed just after midnight. Geneva, Ingrid, and Allie had all managed to stay awake for the entire flight and were ready for bed. Drake, on the other hand, had slept on and off, lulled to sleep by the constant drone of the airplane's engine. Used to only seven hours of sleep a night, he was all ready to start the day.

"What's up with you?" Geneva asked as she slipped into bed and covered herself with a blanket.

"I'm too pumped up. I'm going out for a walk," Drake said.

"Hold on, I'll come with you."

Drake wanted to argue, but Geneva held up her open hand to stop him. She folded the covers back, got out of bed, and dressed within five minutes. Together, they slipped from the room and quietly left the small hotel.

The chill of the early morning air assaulted the couple as they stepped away from the entrance and walked along the ancient sidewalk. Drake reached out for Geneva's hand. It felt warm and inviting in his hand.

"Where are we headed? To find that geocache Ingrid mentioned?" Geneva asked.

Drake considered it for a moment, then sensed a shiver from Geneva. "No. Let's just go around the block. I'll get a little fresh air, then we'll head back."

Geneva nodded. "It's a little nippy out here. I should have brought a warmer coat."

Drake drew Geneva closer to him, hoping some of his body heat would transfer to her, but her shiver said otherwise. He stopped when they got to the corner of the block.

Drake faked a shiver of his own. "Come on, let's go back. I've had enough for tonight, and I'm more tired than I thought I was."

Geneva didn't argue and turned around without another word.

"What are you doing out here?" Drake asked.

"You said you needed to take a walk."

"I did. That explains what I'm doing out here. What are you doing out here?"

Geneva squeezed his hand. "Just thought I'd come along and make sure you stay out of trouble. You know I can't leave you alone. Who knows what trouble you'd get into on your own? Are you good? I'm freezing out here."

Without answering, Drake upped his speed and soon they arrived back at the hotel. Once back in the room, it took Geneva less than two minutes to change out of her clothes and slip back into bed.

Drake took his time going through his before bed ritual, shut off the light, and slipped between the sheets. He put an arm over Geneva and moved close to her.

"Are you awake?" Drake whispered. Beneath his arm, Geneva's rhythmic breathing never fluctuated, and she started to snore softly. Drake moved a little closer to her and kissed her shoulder. "I can't imagine my life without you. You are the only one I'll ever love."

Allie and Ingrid were already in the breakfast room chatting away while eating Frosted Flakes and toast when Drake and Geneva entered.

"Y'all sleep well?" Allie asked as the couple took seats at the table.

"I slept like a rock, and I'm certainly ready to go today," Geneva answered. "Well, I need some coffee, and then I'll be ready."

Ingrid raised her spoon and pointed it toward the back wall. "It's a serve yourself situation. They have cereal, breads, yogurt, and fruit back there."

"You stay here. I'll get you some coffee. You want any food?" Drake asked.

"A bowl of cereal would be good enough, and the coffee, of course. With milk and sugar," Geneva answered.

"I'll take a banana if they have one over there," Allie added.

Drake left the table and headed to the breakfast bar.

"What's going on with him?" Allie asked once he'd gotten out of earshot.

"Why?"

"He's being overly…nice. I mean, he's a good guy, but I've never seen him offer to bring anyone breakfast before."

"Shh. He's returning," Ingrid warned.

Drake placed a small tray on the table overloaded with two bowls of cereal, a mug of steaming coffee, two slices of toast, and a bowl of assorted fruit. He unloaded the tray, returned it to the breakfast nook, and rejoined his friends at the table.

"Are you happy to see me?" Allie asked.

"What?" The question confused Drake, but then he got it. He extracted the banana from his pocket and handed it over.

"I guess not," Allie said as she took the fruit and peeled it open.

Geneva picked up the coffee and cradled the hot mug in her

hands. She inhaled the potent brew, then blew on the liquid to cool it before attempting to take a sip. "My, this is good. Nice and strong. What's on the agenda for today?"

"Not much. Exploring the town, finding some caches, hitting up a couple of museums, and a sunset lake tour," Ingrid said.

"Sounds like a full day," Geneva said.

"What do we have for geocaches?" Drake asked.

"There's that one near here, if you didn't already find it. There's a virtual cache, a mystery, and two multi-caches nearby," Ingrid answered.

"That's it? Only five?"

"For today. Those are the ones that are easily walkable from here. There are plenty of others if we wanted to get in the car and leave town, but we thought it would give us a good taste of what we're in for."

"Are you done with that banana?" Drake asked Allie.

Allie nodded and handed over the half she hadn't eaten. Drake unpeeled the rest and sliced off half-dollar sized sections and let them drop into his cereal. Allie and Ingrid had finished eating and engaged in small talk while Drake and Geneva finished their breakfast. Thirty minutes later, they all stepped into the early morning Italian sun.

"I'll take point," Drake said as he pulled his phone from his pocket and opened his geocaching app. "Closest one is the traditional. It's only a few blocks from here."

Drake led the group along the main road for two blocks, then turned onto a side street.

"Is this right? It looks like an alley," Ingrid said.

Drake checked his app, spun in a circle to make sure he stood in the correct spot, and nodded. "Yep. This is it, the street we need. And notice a half a block down, there's a sign for a shop."

The friends continued up the narrow passageway. The one-way, brick lined lane was just wide enough for two cars, including a parking lane. As they walked, a friendly honk from a passing Fiat encouraged them to stop and move to the side as the vehicle passed.

"How far to the geocache?" Ingrid asked.

Drake stopped, checked the app, and watched as the numbers jumped from three feet, all the way to one hundred, and went back down again. "I'm not sure. There's too much interference from the buildings here. I can't get a good satellite fix."

Geneva looked up and saw the buildings in the lane stood at a minimum of three stories, and most times four, which would easily affect reception.

"Is there a hint?" Geneva asked.

Drake found the info. "Yes. But it's in Italian. Hold on, I'll translate it. Okay. The hint is 'it's piped in'."

"That's not a lot to go on," Ingrid said.

Drake shrugged. "That's all there is. Why don't you two take that side of the street, and we'll take this side?"

Allie and Ingrid stepped ten feet across the lane and started their search. The buildings along the lane shared common walls, making it appear as if a single structure spanned the entire length of the block. Other than doorways and windows, there seemed no place to hide a geocache of any size.

While Drake, Ingrid, and Geneva checked the metal grilles attached to windows for tiny nano containers, Allie strolled up the street, apparently not searching at all. She spotted a metal conduit that ran along the side of a building from the ground to the second floor, stepped off to the side, and found her quarry.

"It's over here."

Allie pulled the small magnetic key holder from behind the pipe, opened it, and retrieved a piece of paper from inside. She added her geocaching nickname just below the last name on the sheet. Allie passed the log to Geneva, the first one to reach her, and waited. Once Drake and Ingrid added their names as well, Allie put everything back together and replaced the geocache where she found it.

"That was easy. What's next?" Allie asked.

Drake glanced at his app. "The virtual and one of the multi-caches are about equidistant from here. Any suggestions?"

"Let's do the virtual," Ingrid said.

"Okay. Let's go."

Drake led the group from the lane, through the streets, and to the Basilica di San Fedele.

"It's beautiful," Allie said when they arrived at the site.

"According to the geocache description, they built it in the late eleven-hundreds," Drake said.

"It's a virtual?" Ingrid asked. "What do we need to get credit for this cache?"

"This is a pretty easy one. There's a door with a dragon on it somewhere here, and we only need to take a selfie with the dragon."

"That's not too bad," Geneva said. "I like those better than answering questions."

"You know where the door is?" Ingrid asked.

Drake shrugged. "Somewhere along the perimeter of this church."

"Can I go inside and look around? Y'all can look for the door while I take a quick peek at the interior, okay?" Allie said.

"Fine by me," Drake said. "The rest of us will find the door, and you come find us when you're done inside."

"Anyone else want to come?" Allie asked.

"I will," Geneva said.

Allie and Geneva walked through the main door and did a quick tour of the chapels inside before approaching the main altar. Allie took a seat in a pew, and Geneva slid in next to her. From her seat, Allie looked around, and enjoyed the views of the frescoes painted on the ceiling above her.

"I really love stuff like this," Allie whispered.

"I didn't know you were religious," Geneva said.

"No. I'm not. But I can still appreciate the artwork and the architecture, right?"

Geneva nodded. "Can you imagine getting married in a place like this? Headed down that aisle with an organ the size of a house playing. With a white dress, a full bouquet of roses, and a train the length of a bedspread."

Allie dropped her gaze and met Geneva's eyes. "Not really. If it ever happens to me, I'd prefer a simple, outdoor wedding. Sounds like this is something you'd go for, though."

Geneva smiled. "Perhaps not this extravagant. But doesn't every woman have the dream of living like a princess on her wedding day and be the center of attention?"

"Center of attention? Now you really talked me out of it," Allie said. "But I'm sure someday your dream will come. Now, let's go find Drake and Ingrid before they move on to the next cache without us."

Allie and Geneva left the church and walked halfway around the perimeter, where they finally caught up with the others.

"It's right over there. Stand by the dragon and I'll take your picture," Drake said.

Allie and Geneva stood on either side of the carving and gave their best smiles as Drake clicked off a couple of photos.

"Did you log it yet?" Geneva asked.

"We did. I'll send you the pic so you can," Drake said.

While Allie and Geneva logged the geocache as found, Drake looked up the next nearest cache and read through the description.

"What's next?" Allie asked.

"It's a four-step multi-cache," Drake said. "The first waypoint is about four-tenths of a mile from here. Should we do that one or look for something less involved?"

Ingrid, Allie, and Geneva huddled together and had a quick discussion without Drake, and after forty seconds, they broke ranks and gave Drake the answer.

"Lead the way," Geneva said.

Drake took Geneva's hand, and the four friends stepped into the street, and soon they made their way along Via Bernadino Luini. The pedestrian traffic had picked up, and they had to navigate around the throngs of people stepping into markets and restaurants. Since the group wasn't in any great hurry, they took their time on the brick-inlaid street and enjoyed the smells emitted from bakeries and stopped occasionally to window shop.

Drake led them straight when the street name changed to Via Pietro Boldoni, and after twenty minutes and a couple of direction changes, the closed in feeling of the cramped streets disappeared when the friends stepped into a piazza. In the center of the square stood a tall, white statue of Alessandro Volta, and Drake guided the group right to it.

"What do we need?" Allie asked.

Drake read the description, then lifted his head, and looked at the giant marble monument. "We need twelve numbers that make up the date and perform some math to come up with the coordinates for the first stage."

Geneva scratched her nose. "Doesn't sound too hard, although I'm not sure how we find twelve numbers for one date."

Ingrid took the initiative and circled the statue. Two minutes later, she returned to the group with her notebook in hand. "Found it. There are twelve numbers because it's in Roman numerals. I jotted them down."

Ingrid passed her pad to Drake, and he passed his phone to Allie. As Allie read what he needed to do to determine the new coordinates, Drake worked on the numbers.

"Got it!" Drake announced.

"Good, let's go," Ingrid said.

"Nope. Hold on just a second. Read me those coordinates, Drake," Allie said. "I'll map them out and see where they lead. If stage two is too far away, we may want to skip it or come back to this one when we're out in the car."

Drake read off the numbers, and Allie mapped it on her phone.

"Yeah. I think you may have made an error there, Duckman," Allie said once she'd seen the results of her plotting.

Drake frowned. "Why?"

Allie turned her phone around. "Because the coordinates you just gave me are somewhere in the Adriatic Sea off the coast of Croatia. Geneva, would you mind?"

Geneva took the pad from Drake and Allie repeated her directions. Within a minute, they had a solution that took them only a quarter mile away. Allie input the waypoint into the phone and handed it back to Drake.

The group took off, and Drake led them from the monument north to Lake Como, then traveled along the lakefront until they reached the European Resistance Monument. While Allie stopped to explore the monument, the remainder of the group found a sign near the marina with the two sets of years they needed for the next step.

"Geneva, if you don't mind, why don't I read the description and tell you what you need to do to get the next waypoint?" Drake said.

Geneva pulled out the notebook and got her pen ready. While listening to Drake, she compared his instructions with the sign and soon had the next set of coordinates ready. Drake entered them into his app and projected the waypoint which wasn't far away.

"How was it?" Ingrid asked, noticing that Allie had returned to them.

"Both amazing and sad at the same time," Allie said. "They have stones from concentration camps and Hiroshima. There are also metal plates inscribed with excerpts of letters written by people sentenced to death during the war. Can you imagine how horrible that must have been?" Allie's words trailed off, and she sniffed twice to hold back the tears. She cleared her throat and spoke again. "Did y'all figure out where to go next?"

"Yep. A tenth of a mile that way," Drake said, pointing toward an enormous park.

Drake took Geneva's hand, and the pair walked ahead of Ingrid and Allie.

"Are you doing okay, Allie?" Ingrid asked.

"Me, sure. Sometimes when I visit places like this, I get too wrapped up in imagining what life must have been like. Then I get trapped in my thoughts. I'm sure that's seems silly to you."

"It's not silly to me. Did you forget my family is from Denmark? Although the country tried to stay neutral during the war, the Germans still occupied my country, and they killed many Danes," Ingrid said.

"I'm sorry. That must have been horrible for your family." Allie moved closer and took Ingrid's arm in hers.

"It was. Although I asked many times, my grandparents never spoke of it. Both claimed they were too young to remember that war, but when I would stay with them during the summer, friends of theirs would visit and I'd overhear the stories they told."

"I hope something as terrible as that war never happens again," Allie said.

"Me too. I think I know where we're headed."

"Where?"

Ingrid pointed off in the distance. Allie looked forward and spotted an old black locomotive sitting on a small section of track.

"You're probably right," Allie said.

The pair had fallen behind Geneva and Drake, and by the time they got to the train, Drake was searching for something while Geneva waited for the women.

"What's he up to?" Allie asked.

"He's looking for a plate with a date on it," Geneva said.

"I found it," Drake said. "It was on the back. Here."

Drake handed the pad to Geneva, then read off what Geneva needed to do to get the coordinates. Once she double-checked her work, she gave the numbers to Drake, and soon the party was back on the move.

They followed the stone path through the park until they came to an area where several concrete columns stood.

"Okay, everyone spread out," Drake said when they arrived at ground zero. Near the columns stood several large trees, a sign directing people to the restrooms, and a half dozen green park benches.

Geneva headed straight for the sign. Drake and Allie started inspecting the trees, and Ingrid made for the nearest bench. There, she slipped her Converse from her right foot, picked up the shoe, and examined the inside until she at last found the item that had annoyed her foot for most of the day.

"Where did you come from?" she asked the toothpick-sized stick that had hitched a ride with her. She tossed the stick away, then ran her fingers inside her shoe to ensure she'd gotten everything. Satisfied, she replaced the shoe. By sure happenstance, she looked down and noticed one bolt securing the bench to the ground didn't look the same as the others. She bent, inspected the odd one, and discovered she had found the cache, a tiny magnetic container the approximate size of her fingertip.

"Got it," she yelled to the others.

Ingrid remained where she was as the others joined her. "It's a nano," she said, holding the dark green cache between her forefinger and thumb.

"Nice job. How in the world did you find that?" Geneva asked.

Ingrid shrugged. "Either luck or skill, so I'm going with

skill."

# CHAPTER THREE

Drake heard a knock on the door and quickly finished tying his shoe before he answered it. Allie stood on the other side, smiling at him.

"Y'all ready to go?" she asked.

"Sure thing," Drake said. "I'll grab Geneva."

"Get a jacket, too. It might be chilly," Allie said. "We'll meet you outside, okay?"

Drake nodded and closed the door. He grabbed his jacket from the closet, and Geneva's as well, and he waited patiently for her to exit the tiny bathroom.

"Do I look okay?" Geneva asked.

"Like an angel. Come on, the others are waiting for us."

Drake helped Geneva into her coat and held the door as she passed through. As they left the hotel, Drake spotted Allie standing next to a car.

"What's this?" Drake asked.

"It's a taxi, silly."

"No, I meant why don't we take our rental?"

"Ingrid's idea. She didn't want us to drink too much at

dinner and have to drive back. Besides, they have little parking at the restaurant."

Drake didn't argue. Instead, he and Geneva slid into the vehicle where Ingrid sat waiting for them. Allie got in next to the driver, and the cab pulled away from the hotel. It was a fast ride, and a few short minutes later, the taxi pulled over and let the group out at the marina.

"What's this?" Geneva asked.

"Dinner. Let's go. I've been looking forward to this all day," Ingrid answered.

The group walked to the end of the pier, where a hostess graciously greeted them and escorted them to a table next to a wide window on the port side of the boat.

"Is this your romantic cruise?" Geneva asked.

"Yep," Allie answered.

"You said there was only room for two on the boat," Drake said.

Allie grinned. "Did I? I misspoke. I meant there was only space for two on this side of the table. And room for two on that side."

Drake rolled his eyes and shook his head. He looked out the window. His eyes focused on a fishing boat coming in for the evening, the people on board waving as they passed the boat he was on.

"Drake, he asked you a question," Geneva said, tapping him on the shoulder.

Drake's view moved from the lake water lapping gently against the hull to the server standing next to the table.

"I'm so sorry," Drake apologized.

"Could I offer you some champagne, sir?"

"Yes, please. And I apologize, I didn't catch your name."

"It is Luca, sir."

Luca nodded once and left the table and returned two minutes later. From his tray, he handed out glasses of champagne to everyone except Allie, who received a glass of lemonade.

"Here's a toast to great friends and a great vacation!" Ingrid said, raising her glass.

The friends clinked glasses, and each took a sip.

"This is your aperitivo course," Luca said when he dropped off several small dishes filled with green and red olives, nuts, and cheese.

The friends dug in, except for Ingrid, who selected a single cube of cheese from the dish.

"Not hungry?" Allie asked.

Ingrid finished the cheese. "I'm famished. I'm waiting for the good stuff."

From the bridge, a horn tooted and a minute later, the boat pulled away from the dock and headed toward the center of the channel. The friends stared out the window as the boat cleared the marina, then followed the shoreline.

The view outside the window was rich in color. Lake Como contained deep blue water, with white wisps of spray that sprung up as the bow cut across the gentle waves. The majestic mountains wore the deep green coat of late spring, the trees awake after a long winter's rest. On the lowest quarter of the hills nearest the shore, Drake spotted small towns, and higher in the hills, an occasional large villa stood sentry over the water. All the buildings had a similar manner to them regardless of size or purpose, done in shades of white or beige, with roofs of red brown that reminded him of terracotta. Above them, the only mark in the bright blue sky was the white contrail of a passing plane.

After fifteen minutes of small talk, Luca returned and cleared away the empty dishes. He returned with fresh plates for the table, and after everyone had one, he brought out the next course.

"What is it?" Ingrid asked as Luca served.

"This is the antipasti course. I present to you a crostino,

topped with sausage and stracchino cheese."

"I've never heard of that cheese," Allie said.

Luca smiled. "It's made from whole cow's milk and is like mozzarella or ricotta. It is fresh and used no more than three days after it's made. Please, enjoy."

Drake, Ingrid, and Geneva waited and observed as Allie picked up the bread, sniffed it, and took a bite.

Allie moaned, chewed, and swallowed. "Oh, my, that's delicious. I'm a fan. I wonder if we can get that cheese in Nashville."

"If we can't, I'm sure we can ship it in from somewhere," Drake said.

"Excellent. Now stop scrutinizing me. You're making me self-conscious," Allie said just before taking another bite.

The rest of the group ate, and all agreed with Allie that the newly discovered cheese was a keeper. Once they'd finished, Luca returned and replaced the dirty plates with clean ones.

"I wonder what's next," Drake said.

"The *primo piatto*. The first course, sir," Luca answered as he removed the empty glasses. "We normally serve it with a Pinot Grigio, unless you'd prefer something else."

"First course? We've already had two," Drake said.

Luca smiled. "No, sir, consider those pre-courses."

"Could I have some water, please?" Allie asked.

"Of course. Gas or no gas?"

Allie thought for half a second. "No gas, please."

Luca nodded, then left the table.

"Gas or no gas?" Drake asked.

Allie laughed. "Even I knew that one. He was asking if I wanted still or carbonated water. I don't like the bubbles in water, so I asked for still. Like plain tap water."

Luca returned a moment later and served the beverages and made another trip and passed out the next course. "I serve to you potato gnocchi, with a pesto."

Drake glanced at the tiny, pillow-shaped pasta in his bowl. "I'm not typically a fan of pesto," he said, stabbing a sample and eating it. "However, this I'm a fan of."

"It's probably freshly made, and not the jarred stuff from the supermarket," Geneva said.

Drake nodded, and with enthusiasm, cleared the remainder of the gnocchi from his bowl in short order. He downed half of his wine, then wiped his mouth with his napkin.

"That was excellent. I wonder what's next," Drake said.

"I don't know, but I can't wait to find out," Geneva said.

Luca returned and acknowledged the empty dishes and gathered them. "We serve the next dish with a Chianti. May I recommend that for you?"

Drake glanced around the table and saw no dissents from Geneva or Ingrid. "Of course."

He drained the last of the wine and set the glass close to the table's edge for easy retrieval.

Luca left with the dirty dishes and silverware and returned with the wine, and a refreshed glass of water for Allie, and then he appeared with a platter, and as he passed out the plates, he explained the dish. "I present a veal osso buco, served over a bed of mashed potatoes, served with carrots, celery, and onions." Once everyone received a plate, he returned with a small basket of Italian bread, which he placed in the center of the table before he retreated.

Drake searched the table. "He forgot the butter."

Ingrid laughed. "The bread is for the marrow. Watch." Ingrid fished a slice of bread from the basket. Then, with her knife, she removed a bit of marrow from the veal bone's center. She spread it over the bread, then took a bite. "Oh my. I haven't had that in so long I'd forgotten how good it is."

Drake watched as Ingrid finished the treat, then repeated what he'd seen her do. He bit into the bread, then made a sour face, and set the bread next to his plate. "Nope. Not for me."

Ingrid shrugged. "It's an acquired taste."

"I hope we don't eat like this over the entire trip. I'd have to buy new pants," Geneva said as she cut off a slice of veal.

"That's why I brought two pairs of sweatpants along. So that I can eat all I want and not worry about it," Drake said.

"Excellent, I'll borrow a pair," Geneva said.

The conversation remained light as the four ate the main meal, and in the end, nothing remained on any of the four plates except the veal bones and the celery sections that Ingrid skipped.

Drake noticed and smiled. "You'll eat bone marrow, but not celery?"

Ingrid shook her head. "It's a texture thing. I don't like the little strings that break off. They always get stuck in my teeth."

"All is well here?" Luca said as he appeared to clear away the plates.

"That was the best thing I've ever eaten," Allie said. "I don't think I'll eat for days after this."

Luca grinned. "You mean after this entire meal is complete, correct?"

"Wait, what?" Allie said.

"I'll be right back."

Luca left, then returned in short order, and placed a white ceramic tray filled with fruit and cheese on the table.

"What's this?" Ingrid asked.

"The cheese and fruit course. With this, I will serve you a crisp, white wine. My personal favorite, okay?" Luca said.

"Okay," Ingrid said.

"How much more can there possibly be?" Geneva asked.

"Only three more courses to go. A nice panna cotta for dessert, then a coffee service, and finally, a fresh limoncello, which I recommend you take on the deck as you watch the sunset."

By the time the friends finished dinner, pushed away from the table, and made it to the boat's open air upper deck, the sun started to descend. The bright blue sky from earlier in the day faded as the sun did, replaced by hues of peach and lavender.

The captain turned the boat, so it faced west, back toward Como, and pulled back the throttle so they barely moved. A breeze, light as a dandelion wish, traveled through the sky.

The four friends sat on benches at the bow. Below them, the boat lazily cut through the water.

"Check those out over there," Geneva said, pointing off toward the north.

The friends watched as a dozen ducks swooped in mere feet over the boat and landed in the water not far away.

Drake draped his arm over Geneva's shoulder. "This is beautiful, isn't it?"

"Magical is more like it," Geneva whispered. "Did you know about this dinner cruise and not tell me?"

"Nope. This was all Allie and Ingrid's doing. I'm just as surprised that you are."

The boat engines hummed a little louder, and the captain picked up enough speed to adjust the vessel, so the bow pointed directly at the setting sun. From their position, they got the illusion that the orange ball headed directly into the lake, right in the valley's midpoint where the opposing mountains met.

The sky had shifted from the lighter hues, chased by darker blues and purples as the sun descended.

Drake looked toward the shore. The green of the trees was gone, replaced by black of the encroaching night, and across the land, dots of lights appeared upon the shore like the bulbs on a Christmas tree. Even the sounds of daytime seemed to silence as the darkness draped over the lake.

The sun touched the far end of the lake, appearing to dip its first rays into the water, like a hesitant swimmer dipping in a toe to test the temperature of a pool.

As the sun dipped farther into the lake and the sky darkened, the stars emerged, one by one. They looked dim at first, but as the night encroached, they grew brighter, as if someone turned a knob to increase the power.

"Look at those stars," Allie said. "I've never seen the Big Dipper so pronounced."

"Me neither," Ingrid said. "Those stars seem like diamonds pressed into black velvet."

The captain engaged the engines just a bit, and the boat continued its leisurely journey toward the sun, which was half-gone, looking more like an animation than an actual event.

Drake watched as Geneva closed her eyes. "This is no time for a nap," he teased.

"I wouldn't think of it. I'm taking in the serenity of this perfect moment. The cool wind on my cheeks, the scent of the lake, the feel of the rocking boat. Try it."

Drake closed his eyes as well, and experienced all that and, as an added pleasure, the warmth of Geneva's body as they sat hip to hip.

The sun at last took her last gasp of air and dipped beneath the water before them.

"That was amazing," Allie said. "I'm so happy we did this."

Ingrid, Geneva, and Drake all agreed with the sentiment.

"I'm getting chilly," Geneva said. "Should we go back inside?"

"Let's stay a couple more minutes and look at that," Drake said.

"What?"

Drake pointed to Geneva's left. To the south, the moon was starting to spring up from behind the mountain.

"Okay, we can stay a bit longer," Geneva agreed.

"Eh, I've seen the moon before," Allie said, waving her hand as if she could swat it from the sky. She stood and reached for Ingrid's hand. "Come on, Ingrid. Let's go see if they have any hot chocolate, or at the least, any more of that limoncello."

Ingrid took Allie's hand and Drake turned and watched

them head for the stairs.

"I thought Allie didn't drink," Geneva said.

"She's not opposed to it," Drake said. "She just doesn't like to go overboard with it. Why, I don't know. It's a story she's yet to tell me, and I've known her forever."

"At least we always have a dependable designated driver," Geneva said.

"Oh, don't ever call her that. She's happy to do it, but she doesn't like the stigma of being a stick in the mud that comes with it."

"Have you ever seen the moon so bright?" Geneva asked.

Drake took a good, long look. The orb had risen above the shadows of the mountain and glowed brightly in the sky. It looked close enough to touch, and he easily appreciated the different shades of whites, grays, and blacks across its surface.

"No, I don't think I have," Drake said. "Are you still cold?"

"A bit, but I don't mind."

"Let's get downstairs. No sense getting a case of pneumonia the first full day of vacation."

Drake found his feet, and helped Geneva to hers, and together, they made their way to the lower level, where they found Allie and Ingrid back at the table. Both had cordial glasses filled with a light-yellow liquid and mugs of a vibrant scented hot chocolate.

"Bad news, Drake," Allie said. "They don't have the packet stuff with the dehydrated marshmallows like you enjoy."

"What is that then?" Drake asked, pointing at the mug.

"The freshest bit of heaven you'll ever taste."

Drake reached for Allie's mug, and she playfully slapped his hand. "Oh, no, mister. You need to get your own."

Drake looked around the room, searching for Luca. "Have you seen the server?"

"He'll be back any moment," Allie said. She drew the mug to her lips, blew on the hot liquid, and sipped. "Oh, my, I'm getting spoiled."

"That's the whole idea of this dinner," Luca said as he approached Drake and Geneva with a tray topped with mugs. Drake handed one to Geneva and took one for himself.

"Thank you, Luca."

"My pleasure, sir. Do you require anything else?"

Drake smiled. "You wouldn't happen to have a bag of marshmallows in the galley, would you?"

"I'll go check right away," Luca said.

As Luca headed toward the kitchen, Ingrid nodded toward him. "Any chance we could hire him for the week? I think he's the best server I've ever had."

"Thank you, ma'am. I appreciate the sentiment," Luca said. "I was unable to find a bag of them, sir, but I found these."

Luca picked the cover from the dish he carried. Drake looked in and saw several white blocks, each twice the size of the average sugar cube.

"What are those?" Drake asked.

"Marshmallows, sir. Made fresh this morning," Luca said. "Please, try one."

"You're kidding me, right?"

Luca shook his head and handed Drake a pair of tiny tongs, and Drake used them to extract a cube from the dish. He dropped it directly into his mouth. He chewed for a moment, then closed his eyes, and smiled as he swallowed.

"Luca. My man! I think I love you."

Luca's cheeks reddened, and he stayed silent.

"Hey," Geneva said, jabbing Drake in the ribs.

"Sorry dear. I meant to say I love his marshmallows."

"Better, but you're still in trouble."

"Here, I'll make it up to you." Drake used the tongs to extract more of the tender goodies from the dish and dropped two each into each of the mugs. "Thank you, Luca. It's been a pleasure having you with us for the night. Can we offer you a tip?"

Luca smiled and waved his hand in front of him like he was fending off an angry dog. "No, thank you, sir. We include the gratuity within the cost of the cruise. Enjoy those. We should reach the dock in fifteen minutes or so."

Luca gave the group a formal bow, then turned and left the friends to their treats.

Allie sighed. "I'm going to miss that man."

Drake rubbed her back. "I think we all will."

A horn sounded, and Drake looked out the window. The lights of the town twinkled in the distance, and he realized the voyage had come to an end.

"If any bit of our trip turns out as good as this, I'm sure this will be a vacation to remember." Drake said.

# CHAPTER FOUR

"Oh, man, it's early," Drake said to Ingrid as they waited in the hotel lobby.

"If I'm not mistaken, that was your idea, remember? Get out early, and I quote, geocache our faces off." Ingrid said.

Drake took off his Tennessee Titans baseball cap and ran his fingers through his hair. "Perhaps I shouldn't have been so eager. Besides, I hoped to get some push back on that from at least one of you."

"Not going to happen. We billed this trip as a geocaching adventure in Italy, remember? Not a let's sleep until noon every day and then see what there is to see a kind of vacation. If we wanted that, we could have gone to Florida."

"Good point," Drake admitted. "Where's Allie? Is she still in your room?"

"She went to get the car from the parking lot."

Drake frowned. "That's a four-block walk from here. I should have gone with her."

"Why?" Ingrid asked.

Drake hesitated but didn't answer.

"So that you could protect her?" Ingrid asked. "You know how Allie is. If anything, you'd have to protect anyone who hassles her from her."

Drake smiled. "True enough. She's as tough as a grizzly bear when she needs to be."

"Are you talking about Allie?" Geneva said as she joined the others.

"How could you tell?" Drake asked.

"Because you used the words, she, tough, and grizzly bear in the same sentence. Nothing against you, Drake, but if I ever got in a bar fight, I'd want that girl right by my side."

Drake laughed. "Me, too."

From inside they heard a couple of friendly toots from a car horn, and Ingrid stepped to the front window and glanced out.

"She's here," Ingrid said. "Everyone ready?"

Ingrid opened the door and held it while Geneva and Drake left the building and wedged themselves into the red Fiat 500X.

"Good morning," Allie said in a chipper tone. "Everyone ready for a fun day?"

"Why are you in such a good mood?" Drake asked.

"I don't know. Excited to be here? Not bogged down by too much wine? You tell me. Everyone buckled in?"

A chorus of yeses came from inside the subcompact SUV.

"Oh, shoot. I almost forgot Luna," Allie said.

"Luna?" Geneva asked.

Allie reached into her jacket pocket and retrieved her Garmin Nuvi GPS and held it up for all to see. "Luna. What do you call yours?"

"I don't have one of those. I use my phone."

"Ah," Allie said as she attached the unit to a holder, plugged the external cord into the auxiliary power outlet near her knee, and turned it on. "Who's my navigator today?"

"What does all that entail?" Ingrid asked.

"Bring up the geocache on the Nuvi and hit the go button.

Also, help find parking at the final location if need be. Also, make sure I don't go down the wrong way of one-way streets or drive off a cliff. I have a bad habit of not paying attention to the machine as I drive."

"Has Drake done it before?" Ingrid asked.

"Of course. All the time."

"Good. He's experienced. Let's switch seats, buddy."

Ingrid and Drake swapped seats, and they were ready to go. Almost.

"Why aren't we moving?" Drake asked.

Allie looked over at him and raised her eyebrows. "Because…"

"Because someone didn't enter a cache into Luna?" Drake asked.

Allie nodded.

"Who has the list for today?" Drake asked.

Ingrid rummaged through her backpack and produced the paper. "Here you go, Drake."

Drake took the list, glanced at it, and found the geocache in Luna. He pressed the green button, and Allie nodded at him, checked her side mirror, and pulled out into the early morning traffic.

"Twenty minutes to the destination. Where are we headed?" Allie asked.

"A little town called Moltrosio," Ingrid said. "There might be parking coordinates for this one."

Drake looked at the list of geocaches in his hand. "How can I tell? By these extra letters next to the geocache name?"

"You got it," Ingrid said. "Caches with parking coordinates have a P, a virtual cache has a V, a multi-cache has an M, a mystery cache has a question mark."

"That's a nice system," Drake said.

"It should be familiar to you too. I got it from Allie."

"Did you put in the parking coordinates, or the cache

coordinates?" Allie asked.

"Let me double check. Are you good on this road?" Drake asked.

Allie checked Luna and saw she had no turns for eight minutes. "Go ahead."

Drake retrieved Luna and checked for waypoints. He selected the correct one and placed Luna back into the holder. "I've got it now. Headed for the parking coordinates."

"Great, thanks."

Allie continued driving on the two-lane road that ran parallel to the north side of Lake Como. The farther she drove, the higher up the mountain they went. Soon, they came to a split in the road, and Luna directed Allie to take the left path toward the village. To their right, down the side of the mountain, were the blue cool waters of the lake. To their left, a twenty-foot stone wall fortified the mountain above them.

"Parking should be another half mile straight, then turn left," Drake said, taking the lead from Luna.

"Heard," Allie said, not taking her eyes from the road. When she got to within a hundred yards, she slowed, noticed a blue and white parking space, and pulled into a spot. "Where's the cache from here?"

"A block back the other way," Ingrid said.

"Okay. Everyone out," Allie said.

The group exited the Fiat, checked traffic, and walked in the direction from which they'd come. There, on a side street, they discovered a tall stone wall.

"Well, I guess it's time to get looking," Drake said.

The four spread out, and each started to search a three-foot-wide section of wall. Allie stood back a foot from the wall and scanned each crevice without touching it. Whenever she spotted something that appeared suspicious to her, she touched it, and attempted to extract it, but she found nothing but stone.

Ingrid, who stood to Allie's left, used a similar method, but she checked far more spaces than Allie did. Although she examined twice as many places, she found nothing either.

Geneva watched Ingrid and Allie for a moment. She rummaged through her backpack until she found a cheap ballpoint pen. Geneva removed the cap, turned it upside down, and ran the plastic clip along the joints in the stone. She quickly traced around the edges of one stone after another, and halfway down the wall, an inch above her knee, she felt something give.

"I think I have something here," Geneva said. She crouched and ran her pen clip into the joint again. With a little finesse and a bit of determination, she removed the small item from the wall.

"What is it?" Drake asked.

Geneva held up a small three-inch by two-inch flat plastic bag wrapped in black duct tape. She opened one end and removed the small plastic log. She signed it and passed it around. Once everyone had their nicknames on the sheet, Geneva put the cache back together and set it back into the wall.

"Nice job, girlfriend," Drake said. He kissed Geneva, took her hand, and began the walk back to the car.

"Can we stop for gelato?" Allie asked as they passed the shop. Allie stopped in front of the window and gave a friendly wave to a worker inside.

"That depends on whether you want to stand there drooling in the window for two hours," Ingrid said.

"Huh?"

"That's when the shop opens, dear."

Allie stepped away from the window and pushed her lower lip out in a pout. "Can we stop on the way home?"

"I think we can manage that," Drake said. "Come on, let's go. The faster we finish the day, the quicker you get your treat."

"Back to the car, everyone!" Allie joked, then took off in a slow jog toward the parking area.

"Where are we going next?" Allie asked as she started the car and the others buckled up for safety.

Drake consulted the list. "Hey Ingrid, why are there two letter Ps here?"

"It probably has two different parking areas," Ingrid answered. "What's the cache and I'll check out the description."

Drake gave her the number, and Ingrid looked up the details of the cache on her phone. "Yeah, okay, there are two sets of parking coordinates for two different trailheads. Do you want to have more or less of a hike?"

"I'd vote for less," Geneva said.

"Then go with the set that ends with three hundred."

Drake scoured through Luna until he found the correct set of coordinates. He entered them in, and they were finally good to go.

Allie followed Luna's directions as they left the village. Two miles from town, Allie turned north and followed a series of switchback roads that climbed higher into the mountains, then back down into a green valley, flushed with clover and livestock. The road traversed the valley, and near the end, they came to a crossroads. There, Allie stopped the car and shifted into Park.

"What's going on?" Drake asked.

"There's a geocache near here. Look." Allie pointed at Luna. There, on the screen, not far away, was a small blue square that showed a waypoint. "Should we do this one first, then move on?"

"Which one is it?" Drake asked.

Allie pushed the box, the name displayed on the screen, and Allie read it to Drake.

"That's about six down on the list. Ingrid, I thought y'all put these in some sort of order."

"I did. Luna's route from the last cache must have differed from the one I mapped out manually," Ingrid said.

Drake nodded. "I get it. Happens all the time back home. Should we go after this one first, then?"

"Might as well, since we're here," Geneva answered for the group.

Allie shrugged, then pushed the button. Luna recalculated, and instead of heading straight, had Allie turn right at the crossroads. After a mile they ascended another mountain, and when the road turned from a two-lane, well-maintained road, to a gravel road that looked wide enough to accommodate only a car and a half, Allie stopped again.

"Are we sure about this?" Allie asked.

Drake glanced at Luna. "It's only another half mile. We've come this far, might as well go the rest of the way."

Allie shrugged. "Okay, then. Here we go."

Allie put the car back into gear and drove. For the first three-tenths of a mile, it was smooth going, but once they got to the edge of a meadow and into tree cover, the road climbed dramatically, like the initial climb of a roller coaster. Allie, unrealistically afraid she'd start sliding backwards, kept feathering the gas and climbing higher. The gravel road turned into dirt tire tracks with a strip of grass in the middle. When they had nearly gone up as far as they could, the road veered to the left and ended abruptly where a downed tree blocked the way.

Allie looked at Luna, which proclaimed they only had sixty feet until they reached their intended destination.

"I guess we walk from here," Allie said. She put the car in Park and turned off the car. After a second of hesitation, she applied the parking brake as well.

"That was a fun little hill," Ingrid said.

"You're more than welcome to drive the way back," Allie said, holding up the keys.

Ingrid shrugged. "Wouldn't be a problem. The way back from somewhere is always easier somehow."

Allie nodded. "True enough. Let's go. Drake, you got a bead on this one?"

Drake had his phone open and brought the geocache up on his app. "Yep, it's that way," he said, pointing in the same direction Luna wanted to go.

The four walked around the fallen tree and followed the remainder of the road until the claustrophobic trees opened and they found themselves at the top of the mountain, with a bright blue sky overhead.

"Oh wow, look at that!" Geneva exclaimed, pointing straight ahead.

She needn't have spoken, since all four friends were standing shoulder to shoulder, all looking in the same direction at the remains of a stone structure a hundred feet ahead of them.

Drake checked his phone. "I think they hid the cache at the building."

"You sure it's safe to go into an old building like that?" Geneva asked.

"I hope so," Drake said.

Drake looked at the stone structure, which, to him, appeared to be the remains of an ancient one-story house. From where he stood, he saw only the back, which contained a single cutout for a small window, and one side, which was nothing but stone. All around the building, the spring grasses were already growing tall around the foundation, and nature completely covered one corner in a blue-green moss.

"Let's check it out," he said.

He took three steps toward the building before the women followed him, and it didn't take long to close the distance. As they got to the corner, Drake reached out and brushed his fingers against the wall.

"I wonder how old this is," he said.

They moved around to the other side and discovered a doorway with no door, and Allie took the lead and stepped into the space. In its day, the interior of the home must have seemed shrouded in darkness considering there was but a single door and a small window for light, but since the house had no roof, the bright sun fully illuminated the inside.

The single room was perhaps fifty feet in length by twenty

feet wide, and except for a built-in fireplace and a pile of brown leaves in one corner, it was completely empty.

Drake stepped to the fireplace, crouched, and brushed some dirt away from the hearth.

"There's some writing here, cut into the stone. It says CNG 1630."

"1630?" Geneva asked. "Someone built this place ten years after the Mayflower left for the New World? That's amazing."

"Or it could be this is even older, and that's just graffiti," Drake said.

Geneva rolled his eyes at him. "Funny. Where's the cache supposed to be?"

Drake checked the app. "Within 20 feet of here. Probably right here in the fireplace." Drake returned his attention to the fireplace, and although he found several loose stones that he could move that provided for potential hiding places, he found nothing but four hundred years' worth of soot and dirt. "Not here."

"Is there a hint for this one?" Ingrid asked.

Drake stood and clapped his hands to remove the loose dirt. He dug the phone from his back pocket and checked it. "It's in Italian. Can you translate it, Ingrid?"

"I could if I were Italian, but I've never studied the language," she said.

Ingrid retrieved her phone, and a single glance confirmed her suspicions. "I've got no cell service up here, so I won't be able to run it through a translator. We'll just have to try finding it the old-fashioned way by looking for it. I'll start on the outside."

As Ingrid left the building, Allie, Geneva, and Drake searched the inside, but other than the fireplace, there was no other place to look. Even the floor comprised hand cut flat stones, and Drake did a quick walk around seeing if there was a loose one, but there wasn't.

"Got to admit, whoever built this did a great job for it to stand for four centuries," Geneva said.

"Except for the roof, of course," Drake said.

"My guess is that they made it from wood or thatch and rotted away or burned off a long time ago," Allie said. "I'm going to go check on Ingrid."

Allie left the house and spotted Ingrid a few feet ahead, sitting in the grass.

"Hey, what are you doing?" Allie asked as she approached her friend.

"Looking," Ingrid answered.

"I don't think you're going to find the cache this way," Allie teased.

Ingrid pulled at Allie's arm. "Sit down here with me," she said.

Allie sat on the ground next to Ingrid, legs crossed. She leaned over, extracted a rock from beneath her, tossed it aside, and reset her position.

"Okay, now look," Ingrid said, pointing out ahead of her.

Allie stopped for a moment and for the first time since they'd arrived, gazed out across the horizon. From where they sat, they had an open view of the entire valley below them. Green patches in various shades cascaded across the valley. Wildflowers that ranged in color from red to yellow to purple provided contrast to the growing grass. The mountains surrounding the valley were alive in green, except for one small patch to her left that looked to be the remains of a wildfire. The tallest peak she saw had a cap of white at the top.

"It's beautiful here," Allie said.

Ingrid nodded. "Can you imagine finding this place, then building a home here? Especially back when they built this home? No technology, fewer people. Nothing to do but survive. Find food, water, shelter. I'll bet they had a small garden up here somewhere. And I'll bet they sat right here at some point every day and just enjoyed the splendor of this view."

Allie stayed silent for a moment, then agreed. "It's one of

the things I like best about geocaching, finding out of the way places like this that time forgot. Magnificent views like this, forgotten history. Those are the real treasures to find."

A small plastic box appeared in Allie's line of sight, and she looked up and saw Geneva standing over her. "Are you two sitting down on the job?"

"Just enjoying this view," Allie said.

Geneva looked out toward the valley, then took a seat next to Allie. "It's spectacular, isn't it?" Geneva opened the box, retrieved the log, signed it, and passed it to Allie, who passed it to Ingrid. Once it returned to Geneva, she returned it to the box, and set the box in the grass next to her.

"Where's Drake?" Allie asked.

"Still looking for the cache inside the house. He's convinced it's in a secret wall somewhere."

"Where did you find it?"

"In the old dead tree on the far side of the house."

"Should we tell him you found it?" Allie asked.

"In a bit," Geneva said. "For now, I'm just enjoying the company and the view."

"Good plan," Allie agreed.

# CHAPTER FIVE

"I think we're in Switzerland," Drake said.

"What? Why would you say that?" Geneva asked.

"Because we passed a sign that said welcome to Switzerland. Ingrid, did you put and Swiss caches on the list?"

"We talked about that. It wasn't all that far away, and none of us have ever geocached in Switzerland before, so one or two may have slipped onto that list."

"Oh, good," Drake said. "For a moment, I thought we were in trouble. You good over there, Allie? Need me to drive?"

Allie glanced at Luna to get her bearings and over at Drake. "No. I'm good. We'll be at the waypoint in just under fifteen minutes."

Allie slowed, turned off the highway, and onto a local road. She followed the valley for six miles, then saw a large metal gate extending across the road. "Hey Ingrid, what does this sign mean?"

"I can't read it from back here. What does it look like?"

"It looks like a red-letter O with white space in the middle," Allie said.

"Is there anything inside the white part?"

"No."

"Okay. That means no entry. The road is closed," Ingrid said.

"And that would explain the big metal gate as well," Drake said.

"How far is the cache from here? Can we walk it?" Geneva asked.

"It's another five miles to the parking coordinates," Allie said.

"And another quarter of a mile after that to the cache," Drake added. "Should I put in the other parking coordinates?"

"Might as well give it a try," Allie said. "If we can't get to that parking area, we'll talk about skipping this cache."

Drake reset Luna while Allie did a U-turn and backtracked to the main road. She turned left and headed into the heart of the Swiss Alps. After fifteen minutes, Luna told her to turn left, and Allie found herself back on a local road. It wound itself around the base of a mountain and afterward followed a river for several miles. Another right turn, and they began to ascend on another series of switchbacks.

"Are you doing okay?" Drake asked Allie after several minutes of watching her.

"I'm fine. Why do you ask?"

"You're driving in the middle of the road ten kilometers an hour under the speed limit, and your knuckles are white. Relax, it's only a mountain."

Allie exhaled. "I guess I'm a little stressed. I don't really like the big ones." Allie inched back into her own lane, then took her right hand off the wheel and flexed her fingers.

"Simply pretend you're back home driving through the Smoky Mountains. You've done that a million times with no problem."

Allie flexed her left hand. "Yeah, but I know that road pretty well. It's always a touch intimidating when you don't recognize the road."

"You drove us through that canyon in New Mexico once. And through the Colorado Rockies, and it snowed during half of that trip," Drake said.

"That's true. That wasn't as bad, though."

"Why not? It's the same thing. Except this road is nice and dry. It's a nice day out, and there's hardly any traffic."

Allie smiled. "Thanks for the words of encouragement. I'm fine now. I got in my own head for a bit, and we're almost there."

"As long as this road isn't closed, too," Ingrid said.

"Thanks for giving me something else to worry about," Allie said. She looked in the rear-view mirror and saw Ingrid smile and wink at her.

Luna ordered a left turn, and Allie pulled into a wide-open parking lot.

"We made it!" Allie said.

"Excellent," Drake said. "I'm ready for a little walk."

"How far is the thing from here?" Geneva asked.

Drake did a quick check. "About over half a mile as the crow flies, but I'm guessing it's hidden off one of the park trails, which, of course, are never in a straight line."

"Trails?" Geneva asked as she exited the Fiat.

Drake pointed to the informational sign he spotted nearby. There were several trails displayed on the map, with corresponding colors to designate how difficult they were.

Once she left the car, Ingrid stepped over to the sign and looked at it.

"It would be nice to understand what that says," Drake said.

"Well," Ingrid started, "don't leave the marked trails. Don't gather any plants, including flowers or mushrooms. There's also don't hunt or disturb the animals or fish."

"How would you disturb a fish?" Drake asked. "Play loud music?"

Ingrid ignored him. "Don't make any fires. Don't bring animals into the park, including dogs. We can't use tents or stay in the park overnight, and we have to pack out all our waste. There's a five hundred Swiss franc fine for violations."

"How much is that in American dollars?" Drake asked.

"Close to six hundred," Geneva answered.

Ingrid kept reading. "Also, regarding the colors, the yellow is a regular trail that anyone should be able to handle. The red trail is a mountain trail on which you should wear your hiking boots, and the blue is the alpine trail which would probably kill us in our current physical conditions."

"Wait a second, Ingrid. I thought you didn't understand Italian," Drake said.

"I don't." Ingrid pointed at a specific part of the sign. "But that's in French, and that I learned as a child."

"The terrain on this cache is only two and a half, so should we assume it's off of a yellow trail?" Allie asked.

"Probably a good assumption," Geneva said. "Ingrid, can you figure out where we are on that map and where the yellow trail runs?"

"Of course," Ingrid said, putting her finger on the map. "There's a little X with the words 'you are here'. If I have the orientation figured out correctly, the trailhead for the yellow trail should be right behind us."

Drake left the board, walked across the parking lot, and surveyed the area. He returned within a few minutes. "Yeah, she's right. There are yellow trail markers over there."

"So, about a mile round trip. Shouldn't take us more than an hour, right? Everyone okay with that or want to stay in the car?" Allie asked.

"Nope. I'm good to go," Ingrid said.

"Me too," Geneva and Drake said simultaneously.

Allie glanced over at Ingrid. "Oh, boy, they're talking in unison now."

Ingrid grinned. "I know. How gross! Come on, let's go track down that cache before they go into full-on cute mode."

Ingrid and Allie turned and headed for the trail.

"Wait for us!" Drake called after them. "Come on, Geneva."

Drake and Geneva broke into a jog and caught up with Allie and Ingrid as they were about to enter the trail, and everyone stopped as they got there.

"Are you going to be able to handle this?" Drake asked Allie. "Looks like it might be a challenge for your bad knee."

"I wrecked that thing two years ago. It's fine. Go. Take the lead. We're burning daylight," Allie answered.

Drake shrugged. "Okay, if you say so. Come single file, though. The trail isn't wide enough for two here."

Drake moved out first, walked for six easy feet, then descended a set of stairs cut into the earth and reinforced with railroad ties. As he moved, he counted them under his breath. When he reached twenty-one, the last stair, he moved forward on the trail, then turned around and waited for the group to catch up to him.

"Looks scary, doesn't it?" Allie said. "Reminds me of those forests in those old-time fairy tales."

Drake looked around and caught what Allie was talking about. All around them, spruce trees that rose like giants from the forest floor dominated the area. The trees cast off the scent that transported Drake back to childhood when they'd go out into the forest every early December to find the year's Christmas tree. The trees littered the forest floor with needles, giving it a spongy feel, like walking on a waterbed.

There were other trees interspersed with the conifers, including clusters of beech, maple, and oak, and a couple Drake couldn't identify by sight alone.

"Should we leave a trail of breadcrumbs?" Geneva asked. Allie waved her GPS in the air. "No need. I've got my handheld on. I marked the car with a waypoint, and I've got the route tracking on, so we'll have no problem getting back here. Much better than breadcrumbs."

Drake moved forward, careful to watch his step to avoid slipping.

"Should have brought hiking poles. I love having one when on a trek like this," Drake said.

"I usually have one too," Geneva said. "Too bad the TSA doesn't allow them as a carry-on item."

"Don't forget to find a spider stick, Drake," Allie said from the back.

"Spider stick?" Geneva asked.

"Drake believes that the entire arachnid species is out to get him and every time he walks through any trees, the spiders run ahead of him and build webs between trees at face height for him to walk into. So, he waves a stick in front of him to knock the webs down before he face-plants into them."

Geneva and Ingrid laughed.

"I'd like to see that," Geneva said.

"You'd like it. He looks like he's conducting an orchestra when he does it."

Drake stopped and turned around. He put his hands on his hips and an angry expression on his face. "Hey, I don't..." he started. He stopped speaking, stepped off the trail, and returned with a length of branch three feet long and two inches in diameter. "See what I found? A perfect spider stick!"

He spun back around and pointed his spider stick in the air in front of him. "Onward!" he directed.

The trail remained flat and straight for a hundred yards, and then they came to a T. Attached to a spruce tree were three arrows. A yellow one pointed right, the red and blue ones pointed left. Drake turned right, and twenty yards later, the trail bent around a boulder the size of the Fiat and started downhill for a short stretch before it leveled out again.

Drake stopped abruptly, and Geneva, not looking ahead of

her at the moment, bumped right into him.

"Hey," Geneva said as she stepped back.

"Sorry. Look at that." Drake pointed his stick ahead of them and off to the right, up the mountain.

"Where?" Geneva asked as she moved closer to Drake.

"See this tree just off the trail here? Follow that like six trees up the hill, then five trees to the left."

The women followed his orders. Ingrid spotted it first.

"What's that?" she asked.

"I don't know," Drake said. "It almost looks like a goat. Why would there be a goat here?"

Allie hadn't seen it yet. "Is it brown and cute and has long horns that curve so far it looks like he could use them to scratch his own back?"

"I don't know about cute, but the rest of it tracks," Drake said.

"It's an ibex." Allie stepped off the trail and moved around Ingrid and Geneva so she could be next to Drake. "Where is it?"

Drake repeated his directions, then pointed directly at the animal. A tree partially obscured the beast, but it moved, and Allie saw it at last.

"That's amazing," Allie said.

"Are they dangerous?" Ingrid asked.

"No. It'll run away if we bother with it too much."

"Anything else we should keep in mind while on this little adventure?" Drake asked.

Allie shrugged. "Just the usual stuff we'd watch for back home. Birds, bears, deer, wolves. The common stuff. Like foxes, hedgehogs, marmots, and chamois."

"What's a chamois?" Geneva asked.

"Looks like that ibex, except with shorter horns," Allie answered.

"What's a marmot?" Ingrid asked.

"Large ground squirrel. Looks a little like a groundhog."

Allie removed her camera from her pocket, got the ibex in the center of the viewfinder, and snapped a picture. "That was an excellent picture. He's looking right at us."

"How do you know so much about these animals?" Drake asked.

Allie took the lead and headed down the trail. "Animal Planet," she said over her shoulder.

With Allie in the lead, she picked up the pace of the group, and walked faster than the casual saunter that Drake had the group traveling by. As she walked, she examined the ground, on the lookout for any outcroppings of rocks, roots, or anything else that would trip them. The part of the trail they currently traversed seemed relatively free of debris and looked well maintained. She led the pack for ten minutes before she stopped and turned around.

"Everyone good yet?" she asked as she fished her water bottle from her backpack and took a drink. No one said otherwise. "How much farther, Drake?"

Drake checked and pointed down the ridge. "Three-tenths of a mile. Not too bad."

"Take point," Allie said.

Drake retook the lead position and marched on, once again slowing the pace. After two hundred feet, he stopped. "We've got a problem here," he said.

"What?" Allie asked.

"Which way do we go?" he asked.

Allie looked around and realized there were two trails ahead of them. One went straight along the ridge, the other snaked down the mountain. She found and pointed to a yellow trail marker three feet straight ahead of them. "Follow the yellow."

Drake stepped onto the other trail, walked four feet, and pointed to another trail marker attached to a tree. It, too, contained a bright yellow coat of paint. "Which one?"

Allie glanced at the marker near her, then at Drake's. "I'm not sure."

"Hold on, let me check the trail map," Ingrid said.

"Where did you get a map?" Geneva asked.

"I took a picture of the one on the sign." Ingrid brought up the gallery on her phone and examined it for a moment. "I don't see the trail on there."

Ingrid handed her phone to Geneva, who took it, looked at it for twenty seconds before she passed it off to Allie. Allie scrutinized the image, stepped away from the group, and faced the direction from which they'd come. Everyone watched as she performed a lot of pointing and pirouetting, and, and last, rejoined the group. She gave Ingrid her phone back.

"I think it's a new trail, and they haven't updated the map yet," Allie said.

"So, which one do we follow?" Geneva asked.

"Where's the cache?" Allie asked.

Drake looked at the phone and lined up the arrow. He pointed in a direction that bisected both trails. "I think this trail does a loop. Why don't we split up, each take a direction, and meet at the cache? Allie, you and Ingrid take the straight trail, which looks easier from here, and Geneva and I will take the other."

"Okay. It shouldn't take more than another ten minutes to find that cache, so let's meet back here in twenty if we don't meet before then," Allie said. "Let's go, Ingrid. We'll beat them to it and get the names on the log first."

"I doubt it. Come on, Geneva," Drake said.

Drake stepped back down to the lower trail and waited for Geneva, watching her as she walked.

"Wait. Why are you limping?"

"It's nothing. I stepped on a rock a while ago and twisted my ankle," Geneva said.

Drake returned to the main trail and saw Allie and Ingrid

had already slipped out of view. "Allie! Come back here!" Drake called. He waited a few moments, then exhaled when they saw them on their way back.

"What's up, buttercup?" Allie asked.

"Geneva broke her ankle," Drake said.

Geneva pushed him aside. "I did not break it. I rolled it on a rock. No big deal."

"Let Allie take a peek at it," Drake said.

Geneva looked from Drake to Allie and finally capitulated. "Okay, fine. What do you need me to do?"

Allie looked around and spotted a downed tree pushed off to the edge of the trail. "Can you make it to that tree and have a seat?"

Geneva turned, and Drake grabbed her arm for support. Allie stopped him.

"Let her do it. I want to see how she moves."

Geneva limped ten feet to the tree, pivoted, and sat. "See. No problem."

"You've got a slight limp," Allie said as she approached Geneva. "Does it hurt?"

"Nothing a couple aspirin wouldn't take care of."

"Can I look at it?"

"Do whatever you need to do to make Drake feel better," Geneva said.

Allie smiled. She crouched and removed Geneva's shoe and sock and examined her foot and ankle. "It's a little aggravated but doesn't seem swollen or broken. I think she twisted it and should be able to walk it off."

"That was the same conclusion I came to. You better now, Drake?" Geneva asked as she put her sock.

Drake nodded. "Just trying to be careful out here. You never know what will happen."

"I'll tell you what. You take Ingrid with you down the harder trail, and I'll take Geneva with me. I'll keep my eye on her and make sure she's okay. If she gets any worse, I'll wait with her here until y'all get back, and then we'll head back to the car together."

Drake nodded. "Sounds like a plan to me. You okay with it, Geneva? Ingrid?"

"Sure," the women said as one.

"Okay. Be good, and don't be afraid to take it easy," Drake said.

Drake nodded at Ingrid, and they stepped back onto the trail and headed down the trail branch he'd found.

"She'll be fine, Drake. Allie will take excellent care of her," Ingrid said as they stepped around a large boulder.

"I know. We'll probably get to that cache and find their names already on it, and them back on that tree, lounging around and waiting for us."

The pair followed the trail as it curved back on itself and down the mountain before it returned to the direction of the cache. The trail was a rough one and contained parts that had them walking across sections of rock, around boulders, over tree roots, and in one case, they needed to climb over a tree that blocked the entire path.

After fifteen minutes of walking, Drake stopped and wiped the sweat from his forehead.

"Ever go out for a cache you later regret?" he asked.

Ingrid nodded. "You mean like this one?"

Drake smiled. "Come on. We're already running late."

"Should we go back?"

Drake checked his position. "No. We're only four hundred feet away. Let's keep moving forward and hope we pick up the easier trail at the cache."

Drake took his next step just as a rumble of thunder rolled up the mountain. "That didn't sound good."

Drake barely finished his sentence when the rain began. It started as a few lazy drops, then the skies opened, and the deluge began; drenching the pair in seconds.

"Let's go back," Ingrid pleaded.

"It will be faster going straight ahead," Drake said.

He moved forward thirty feet, then stopped.

"What is it?" Ingrid said.

Drake inched over so she could look. A tree had fallen parallel to the trail, leaving mere inches between the path and the edge. Where the path remained, the falling rainwater mixed with the runoff from up the hill, making a small puddle that was growing larger by the second.

"Take it slow through here," Drake said. "Watch how I do this and follow my steps."

Drake took a step, placing his foot as close to the tree as he could, then did the same with the next step. He walked slowly and intentionally, and using his method, he'd already made it halfway past the obstacle.

Lightning flashed above them, followed by a crack of thunder that resembled an exploding bomb. Drake, surprised by the event, wedged his foot underneath an inch of exposed branch. He pulled his foot out too hard. Drake pinwheeled his arms, trying to maintain his balance, but it didn't work. He did an awkward somersault, and disappeared down the mountain, leaving Ingrid alone on the trail.

Ingrid stared at the spot where Drake had stood a second before, and toward where he'd gone. The rain increased in velocity. Ingrid wiped the rain from her eyes and clenched her fists in frustration.

"Shit!" she screamed to the trees.

# CHAPTER SIX

Ingrid stood alone in the rain, undecided on what to do. She remained still for a moment getting drenched, decided on a course of action, and grabbed her phone from her back pocket. She leaned over, attempting to protect it from the rain, brought up her contacts, and attempted to call Allie. Ingrid didn't even need to place the phone next to her ear to determine that the call wouldn't go through. Next, she tried to send texts to both Allie and Geneva and noticed neither one was delivered.

"Shit," she repeated.

Ingrid removed her backpack and dropped the phone inside to protect it from the elements and returned the pack to her shoulders. She turned around and checked out the trail they'd come in on and spotted a full-fledged stream flowing from the mountain above. As she watched, the water streamed faster, blocking her way.

Ingrid faced the other direction and eyed the spot where Drake had gone off the side. The puddle had grown deeper.

Ingrid hesitated, unable to move like a rabbit spotting a distant fox. She wiped the water from her face again, waited until a peal of thunder rose from the valley, and took one step forward. At first, she placed her foot next to the downed tree, just like she watched Drake do. Suddenly, she changed her mind and sat on the tree. An unpleasant sensation attacked her backside, the combination of cold water and rough bark.   Ingrid used her hands to steady herself and slid halfway down the length of the tree, stopping where Drake had gone over the edge. She brushed her hair back with her hand and leaned forward as far as she dared, hoping to catch some sight of Drake.

"Drake? Drake! Can you hear me? Drake?" she screamed down the mountain. She stopped calling and listened for half a minute, but all she picked up was the pounding of raindrops against the leaves and ground.

Ingrid looked to her right and, two inches at a time, moved her away across the remainder of the tree. Once she got across, she struggled to her feet and started jogging up the trail. She made it twenty feet down the path before the toe of her right foot caught a rock, and she splayed forward like a baseball runner stealing second base. Ingrid wasn't running fast, but the mud and water lessened the resistance when she hit the ground. She slid forward, getting a face full of grime and muddying the entire front of her body in the process.  Undaunted, she attempted to get to her feet, slipped once again, and fell onto her backside. Finally, she stood erect, used the bottom of her T-shirt to wipe the mud from her face, and regained her run along the trail.

She ran for fifty more years and stopped when the trail, which she expected to bend off to the right, meandered off to the left instead. Ingrid moved six feet along the path and encountered a steep descent before her.

"Geneva! Allie!" Ingrid screamed. She stopped but heard nothing but rain and thunder in response. She yelled again, and a third and fourth time, each time putting more effort in than the time before. After the fifth time, she retrieved her phone and once again tried to call for help. Ingrid's shoulders slumped when she saw she had no service in the area.

"Shit," Ingrid said.

She put her hands on her hips and looked down the trail again, watching the water flow steadily off the side of the steep hill, taking the path of least resistance.

"Okay, Ingrid, think this out. I've got three choices here. Try to guess where Allie and Geneva are and attempt to head off trail to find them, check where this trail leads and hope it goes somewhere, or go back and try to find Drake. Option one is idiotic. I'd end up getting myself lost, I'm sure. Option two is a long shot, so that only leaves me with option three, which is almost as idiotic as option one."

Ingrid drew in a deep breath, exhaled, and made her way back to the downed tree. Applying the same process she did before, Ingrid sat on the tree trunk and made her way to the center. She looked as far as she could down the mountain, but it wasn't far. All she saw was a muddy patch that resembled a slide, trees, and a dense fog that had appeared since she'd been gone. The gray and white fog rose from below like the boil from a witch's cauldron.

"Drake?" she yelled. "Are you down there? Drake?"

She hoped for an answer from him, or at least a sound other than the constant rain, but no answer came.

"Okay. Let's figure this out," Ingrid said to the universe. "I don't want to go the same way down that Drake did. That seems like a stupid idea, so let's find a better way."

Ingrid looked down to her left. The stream that had blocked her from going back to the main trail had widened, expanded, flooded more trail toward her, and added a second branch to the mini waterfall that dropped from the mountain not far from where she sat. To her right, things looked a little more promising, but only a little. Ingrid backtracked to the end of the trunk, searched for a steady spot to put her foot on, and stepped off the trail.

With care, Ingrid put her weight on the large rock she'd selected and put her left foot next to her right. Below her she discovered a half dozen stones that outcropped like steps, and she cautiously took them, one at a time, testing each one before she fully committed. The last step was two feet behind a large spruce, so her next move was to leave the rock and embrace the tree in a hug. She couldn't see around the giant tree without taking a few baby steps to the left, and once she did, she noticed the fog was getting closer and the next tree was ten feet down the mountain.

The pitch was steep, but not vertical, so Ingrid leaned against the tree and stepped forward. She crouched, took a sideway step down with her right foot, then followed it with her left. Another two steps, and she committed to the plan. The rain picked up a little harder, and she felt her back get pelted with large drops. Ingrid stepped again and the second she applied weight, the wet pine needles beneath her feet shifted. Ingrid fell on her hip, and she screamed as she slid the rest of the way until she slammed feet first into the tree she'd been aiming for.

The impact jarred the scream from her throat, and she worried she'd miss the tree and tumble down the valley, but she stopped when she slammed into the trunk. Ingrid rolled onto her back, moaned, and rubbed the hip she'd landed hard on. Without looking, she assumed the rough ride had torn her pants, and when she glanced at her fingers, she noticed bright red blood that washed away one raindrop at a time.

She gritted her teeth and slowly got back to her feet, battered but not broken. The tree she'd crashed against was only half as wide as the previous one, so she held on easily while she looked around it. Eight feet below her looked to flow a two-foot-wide stream produced by the heavy rain that ran parallel to the hill she found herself on. Two feet past the stream was the next drop off down the mountain, and below that, she couldn't tell, since the fog was almost at that level.

Ingrid stood stone still for a moment, considering her best option forward, and as she did, an ibex came along, walking from left to her right as if out on a summer stroll.

"Son of a bitch," Ingrid said. "It's a deer path."

The ibex spotted Ingrid, looked in her direction and took off running.

Ingrid sat on the wet ground and pushed out from the tree, her heels digging into the earth. She released the tension in her legs, slid a foot down the mountain and dug her heels in again to stop her momentum. Slowly, she descended until at last her feet hit the path. Once she was down, she stood, then, having a flat surface to tread on, followed the path until she came to a ten-foot drop that resembled a mud waterfall.

"I'm guessing you went that way, Drake," she said knowing full well he wouldn't respond.

Next to the path was a broken sapling. Ingrid looked as far down the hill as she could before the fog obscured her view. Three quarters of the way below her, she spotted other saplings the same size as the one next to her.

"Okay. I hope this works," she said.

Ingrid rubbed her hands on her pants and grabbed the sapling and tugged. It hadn't broken all the way through, so although she expected it to snap off in her hands, it didn't. She moved toward the edge of the cliff, and using the sapling as a makeshift rope, descended. When she got close enough to reach a sapling that wasn't already bent in half, she transferred from the original one. Ingrid held tight to the new tree, then used it as a guide until she reached the next one. The second sapling led to a third, and before she knew it, Ingrid found herself on top of a rock outcropping. She got onto her stomach, crawled to the edge, and peered over. From where she was, she couldn't see a thing with the deep fog.

Ingrid moved to the side of the ledge and found it connected with the mountain and sloped down. Watching her step as she proceeded, she stepped from place to place until she found herself on yet another deer trail. When she turned around and looked behind her, she realized the outcropping she had been laying on top of moments earlier was actually a cave. Cold, wet, sore, and tired, she stepped inside the cave a few feet to get out of the rain.

"Hello?" she said into the cave. "Anyone in here?"

Ingrid heard nothing except her voice echoing back at her. The cave cut into the mountainside far enough that Ingrid didn't see the back of it, but having no desire to explore, she instead selected a large rock and sat down.

"Okay. I'll rest for a minute, and then get back at it," she said aloud.

Ingrid watched the rain fall outside the cave for a moment and shivered when a cold breeze wrapped its essence around her. She took her backpack from her shoulders, retrieved her phone, and checked to see if she had any service or if any of her messages had gone through. The answer being no to both, Ingrid placed it back in her backpack. As she zipped up the bag, she caught sight of her hands. They looked wrinkled and white, and she had a cut on her left hand that ran from the base of her thumb all the way to the wrist.

"There goes my career as a hand model," she said as loud as she could, trying to get a response from someone who wasn't there.

She yawned and stretched, trying to work the knots from her spine.

"I should have stayed in bed. Okay, girl, let's do this."

With a groan, Ingrid pushed herself to a standing position and then stepped into the cave's mouth. She stopped for a moment, not wanting to leave the relative comfort of the dry cave, took a deep breath and stepped out into the elements. She turned left and followed the deer trail. After fifty yards, Ingrid found Drake's waterfall, and she got close to the side, and leaned over. She expected to see rocks, trees, random puddles, and mud, but she missed a breath when she spotted a Titans blue baseball cap hanging from a short branch like someone had placed it there. The cap dangled only four feet from her, and the terrain gently sloped, so she easily stepped down to the hat and plucked it from the tree.

She turned the hat over in her hands. Other than being dirty and wrinkled, it didn't look like it had just fallen off a mountain. Ingrid inspected the inside and found it to be relatively clean. She brushed her hair back with her hands, then put the cap on and pulled the bill low to protect her eyes from the rain.

"Drake? Drake, can you hear me?" Ingrid yelled.

She paused. Nothing. Ingrid repeated the calls over and over again, waiting for a response in between, but nothing answered but storm sounds.

"Dammit, Drake," Ingrid said as she stepped down the slope. For twenty-five feet, she followed the impromptu stream as it veered gently to the left, then it disappeared from sight. Ingrid crept to the edge and peered over. Although the fog still swirled, she estimated the drop was at least thirty vertical feet. She shuddered, happy she couldn't see what was waiting for her at the bottom of the drop, but she knew she had to get down there.

Ingrid moved away from the edge, intending to find a less dramatic way to the bottom. As she stepped around a spruce, her foot caught on something, and she crashed to the ground. She got to her hands and knees, then pushed herself up and stood. Ingrid brushed the pine needles and dirt from her hands, then turned to see what she'd tripped over.

It was a leg, and attached to the leg was the rest of Drake, sitting with his back to the spruce tree. Ingrid stepped over and dropped to her knees before him.

"Drake? You alive, buddy?"

Ingrid grabbed Drake's arm, felt for a pulse, and found it

beating steady and strong. She tapped gently on his right cheek as she repeated his name.

Finally, his eyes opened. "Hey, you. What took you so long to find me?"

Ingrid shrugged. "You know me. I like to take my time with things."

It took quite an effort, but Drake smiled. It faded quickly from his face.

"How are you doing?" Ingrid asked.

"That was the worst water slide ride ever," Drake said, his voice weak.

"Anything broken?"

Drake's eyes shut again. Rather than wake him right away, Ingrid gave him a rough inspection and checked his extremities and head for injuries.

"What are you going, Allie?" Drake muttered.

"It's Ingrid. I'm not going anywhere. I'm checking you for broken bones."

"Under shirt," Drake said. He tried to pull his shirt up but he didn't have the strength.

Ingrid lifted his shirt for him.

"Holy shit!" Ingrid exclaimed when she saw the three-inch piece of wood sticking out of Drake's stomach, just left of his navel. It was as thick as her thumb. She took it between two fingers to check the resistance, and it refused to come out easily, so Ingrid left it alone and replaced Drake's shirt.

"How bad is it?" Drake asked.

"I wouldn't want one. Drake, listen to me. I can't leave you here alone. We need to get you out of this rain. I know a place not far from here, but I can't carry you. You'll have to walk, okay?"

Ingrid looked at Drake's closed eyes and assumed he'd passed out again. She prepared to tap him on the cheek when he answered.

"Okay. We should go slow. It's slippers out there," he

mumbled.

"That's right, Drake, slippers out here indeed. Can you open your eyes?"

Ingrid waited.

"Drake?"

Drake's eyes fluttered but failed to open.

Ingrid crouched and got close to Drake's ear. "Drake!" she yelled with all her might.

Drake's eyes snapped open as if spring-loaded. He shook his head, confused. "What?"

"Come on. Time to get up. Let's go."

Before Drake could answer, Ingrid grabbed his belt and started to lift him. Although she wasn't strong enough to pull him to his feet, he got the idea, struggled to get his feet beneath him, and stood. Ingrid propped him against the tree and held onto his belt so he wouldn't fall.

"You see me, Drake?" Ingrid asked.

"Yes," he mumbled.

"Here's the plan. We're going up that little hill, then we're going to take a path to a cave I found. It's no more than three hundred feet, okay? And once we get going, we're not going to stop. Got it?"

Drake nodded.

"Tell me the plan, Drake."

Drake raised his arm halfway and pointed up the mountain. "Go up the hill, then path, then cave."

"Right. And no stopping. That's the important part.  We're going on the count of three, so put your arm around my neck."

Drake did as he was told, and Ingrid counted. At three, she pulled him away from the tree. Drake's full body weight rested on Ingrid's shoulders, and she felt him pulling her to the ground.

"Hey, come on, man, move your feet."

Drake did, reluctantly, the left foot first, then the right. It wasn't more than a shuffle, but they moved, and as a bonus, he held his own weight.

"Let's get out of the open," Ingrid said. By using his belt more like a guide than for support, Ingrid prompted him to walk with her, and to her surprise, they ambled up the soft slope and made it to the deer trail in just over twelve minutes. Ingrid's back ached from supporting most of Drake's weight, but she said no breaks, so she needed to stick to that plan. She knew if she let him sit now, it would take more effort than she had in her to get him off the ground again.

"Come on, it's not much farther," Ingrid said. "Fifty more steps, Drake. You can do it."

Drake murmured something Ingrid couldn't pick up. Instead, she stepped forward and pulled him along the best that she could, but eventually she worked into a rhythm. Step, pull. Another step, another pull. Using her improvised method, one foot traveled turned into a yard, and then another. Ingrid desired to pick up the pace, but had neither the strength nor Drake's cooperation, so she kept it nice and easy. One yard at a time. Step. Pull. Step. Pull.

At last, they reached the cave opening, and Ingrid helped Drake inside. She considered setting him on the rock she's sat on earlier, but didn't want him to fall over, so instead she opted to sit him down on the ground with his back against the wall.

Ingrid took off Drake's hat, set it in his lap, and ran her fingers through her long hair, squeezing the water from it as she did. She looked at Drake, who was unconscious again.

"Okay, you're right. Let's rest up for a moment before we decide what to do next," she said as she closed her eyes.

# CHAPTER SEVEN

"Where do you think they are?" Allie asked, shifting in her seat to attempt to get more comfortable.

"It beats me," Geneva said. "You don't think they're waiting back at that tree you said we'd wait by, do you?"

"I would hope not. It wouldn't make sense to stand out in this downpour when we could hang in the nice dry car."

"Speaking of nice and dry, would you mind turning on the heat?" Geneva asked.

Allie glanced at her friend in the passenger seat. Geneva's hair was wet, and her forehead glistened like she'd recently come out of the shower.

"Of course." Allie started the car, turned the heat to the maximum setting, and adjusted the vents so the upcoming warm air blew on them. "This good?"

Geneva adjusted the vent closest to her. "Yes, thank you. What's the plan now? We sit and wait?"

Allie watched the rain buffet on the windshield. She activated the wipers, and they did their job momentarily, but in the short time between when they rose and fell again, the windshield got covered with twice as much water.

"Is it me, or is this rain like going through a car wash?" Geneva asked.

"I had that same image run through my head, complete with that massive rotating brush overhead. I'm not sure what we should do. Wait for the rain to taper off? Go out and try to find them? How long have they been gone?"

Geneva checked the time on her phone. "It's been an hour since we've been back, and it probably took us what, a half hour hike from when it started raining?"

Allie nodded. "Sounds about right."

"So, where do you imagine they are?" Geneva asked.

"I really don't have the faintest idea. At best, they found some shelter and hunkered in until the rain lets up. At worst…"

"No need to give me the worst case."

Allie patted Geneva's knee. "Stop worrying. I'm sure they're fine."

"Yeah, but doesn't Drake have a habit of getting himself into trouble?"

"Oh, trust me, he does. He'll do some extremely questionable things when looking for a geocache, but to his credit, he's never put anyone else's safety in jeopardy. He wouldn't do anything stupid with Ingrid in tow," Allie said.

"I know. I'm only getting nervous for both of them."

"Me too."

"We should try calling them again," Geneva said, holding up her phone.

Allie dialed Drake, noticed the call never connected, and tried Ingrid and received the same result. Next, she tried sending messages to both, and shook her head when those didn't go through, either.

"Did you have any luck?" Geneva asked.

Allie shook her head. "Nope. The call I made to you didn't go through, either, and you're sitting right next to me."

"I understood these international phone plans we got were supposed to work everywhere," Geneva said.

"I don't think it's the plan. My guess is it's the location. I can't imagine there's a lot of coverage where we are," Allie answered.

"So, what are we going to do if we need help? Drive down the mountain?"

As much as she hated the prospect of driving all the way back to town in the pouring rain, Allie didn't see another solution. "I guess so. But I don't like the idea of leaving here until we have to. I'd hate it if Drake and Ingrid came up the trail and found this parking lot empty."

The friends stopped talking. Other than the patter of rain on the windshield and roof, and the constant hum of the heater, silence settled over the car like a blanket. After a few minutes, the thermostat ticked, and the car got warmer inside. Allie flipped on the radio, found nothing to listen to, and switched it off again. To amuse herself, she tapped out a rhythm on the steering wheel.

"That's super annoying," Geneva said.

Allie stopped in mid-beat and looked over at her friend. "Sorry. I don't know what to do with my hands."

"Why don't we give it fifteen more minutes, and we'll go out and look for them?" Geneva said.

Allie looked down at her phone and checked the current time. "Screw that. I'm going now. Do you want to come with, or wait here in the nice warm and dry car?"

Geneva smiled. "Of course, I'd prefer to wait here. But I'll go with you. They're my friends, too. Besides, I don't want you to disappear into the wilderness, too."

Allie exhaled. "Thank goodness. I wasn't looking forward to heading out there by myself. Do you have an umbrella or a rain jacket with you?"

Geneva shook her head. "Not with me. I have both packed away in my luggage back at the hotel."

"And you didn't think to bring them along with us today?" Allie scolded.

"Why would I? The weather looked to be perfect everywhere in the area. I didn't think I'd need them. Anyway, where's your umbrella and rain jacket?"

Allie looked from Geneva, out the side window, and back at Geneva. A smile spread across her face. "In my room, hanging in the closet."

Geneva waved a finger at her. Then both women broke out in authentic, mind-clearing laughter. Once she finished, Allie turned off the car.

"You ready to do this?" Allie asked. "I mean, are you sure you can make it with that ankle? We barely made it back here the last time."

Geneva let loose a loud sigh. "I need to try. I can't sit here and do nothing."

Allie shook her head. "No. I'm serious, Geneva. If that ankle is going to be a problem, then you shouldn't go. If we got halfway down the trail and it gave out, that wouldn't do any of us any good."

"I tell you I'm fine," Geneva said. "The second my foot starts to bother me, I'll come right back to the car. Honestly."

Allie looked her in the eyes, then nodded. "Okay. Any problem and you come right back."

Allie and Geneva reached for the door handles at the same time, popped open the doors, and stepped out in unison.

"Are we taking the packs?" Geneva asked.

"Yeah, we probably should," Allie said. She opened the back door, retrieved both backpacks, and waited for Geneva to get to her, then passed Geneva her backpack. Allie shut the door, locked the car, and shoved the keys into her front pocket.

As one, they turned, stepped across the parking lot, and started down the trail, Allie in the lead. Moving ahead, Allie stepped down the first five stairs, then stopped and turned to wait for Geneva. Allie spotted her at the top, looking like she was trying to negotiate the first step down.

Allie trudged back up the steps and joined Geneva at the top.

"What's going on?" Allie asked.

"I'm not sure," Geneva said. "I thought I could go, but I'm not sure."

"All right let's go back," Allie said.

Allie let Geneva walk ahead of her, and when they returned to the Fiat, Allie had Geneva get in the back seat behind the passenger. Geneva leaned up against the closed door and put her feet up on the seat. Allie removed Geneva's shoe and sock and inspected her ankle.

"It's more swollen than it was before," Allie said. "And it's redder. I still think it's a mild sprain, but obviously you shouldn't be walking around the mountainside in a rainstorm on it. You stay here, and I'll go looking for them."

Geneva reached out and grabbed Allie's hand. "No. I'm not good with you going out there alone."

"I can appreciate that, but someone needs to go. Can you honestly tell me you'd make it even a hundred yards down that trail without doing more damage to that ankle and putting the rest of us at risk?"

Geneva's eyes dropped to her lap, and she let go of Allie's hand.

"Look, Geneva, it's not worth you hurting yourself, too. Remember that fall I took in Arizona? I'm still not fully recovered from that, and that was over two years ago. You need to be smart and stay here. In fact, that's probably for the best. If anyone comes into the parking lot, you can tell them what's going on and see if they can get some help for us, okay?"

Geneva hesitated, then eventually nodded. "Okay, okay. I'll wait here."

Allie helped Geneva back into her sock and shoe and then

propped Geneva's foot up on her backpack.

"Keep your ankle elevated as much as you can. I'll be back soon."

Allie removed the keys from her pocket and held them out for Geneva. As Geneva took the keys, she grasped Allie's hand firmly in hers.

"Be careful, Allie. Please."

Allie nodded, stepped back, and closed the door.

Alone, Allie wandered to the trailhead, took a deep breath, and carefully moved down the steps.

Since it was still raining hard, the trail was a muddy mess in places interspersed with deep puddles. She did what she could to stay out of the water and away from anything on the ground that would cause her to lose her footing. Although it took her twice the time to cover the same ground as before, she eventually made it to the downed tree they had all agreed to meet at a thousand hours earlier.

"Drake? Ingrid?" Allie called out, hoping the pair were within earshot. "Drake! Ingrid!"

Allie turned in a circle, calling out names, listening, then repeating the action until she kept moving. In a few steps she made it to the break in the trail and without hesitation, stepped onto the trail she had last seen Drake and Ingrid on.

In the rain, the lower trail seemed twice as perilous as the upper trail she and Geneva had taken earlier. Half the trail turned into a small, fast-flowing stream fed by rain and gravity, and Allie did her best to avoid the deepest depressions since she knew that once she stepped into a puddle, she really had no idea where she was placing her foot. Allie feared she'd end up in the back of the Fiat with Geneva, sharing a backpack to keep their broken ankles elevated.

The path was no simple walk in the park, and Allie moved with a purpose, checking her footholds, and using the surrounding items, be they boulders or trees, to steady herself.

After many elongated minutes, Allie turned a corner and found herself on a wider trail. The trail seemed flat and relatively free of obstructions and puddles, so Allie picked up the pace and trudged on for a hundred feet before she came to a stop.

Before her, the path was gone and in its place was a torrent of water rushing down from the mountain above her. She looked up and saw that time had eroded away a section of the mountainside and created a funnel that appeared at least twenty feet wide at the top and narrowed down to four feet where she currently stood. The water rushed fast and free before her.

"No way I'm getting across that," Allie said.

Allie stepped as close as she could to the water without getting the tops of her shoes splashed and looked past the water. Through the intermittent fog, she saw the path beyond, and then, a few feet farther on, an area that looked like a mudslide.

"Drake! Ingrid!" Allie called out. She tried to listen, but all she heard was the water racing by at her feet. She screamed the names again, and louder, but heard nothing in return.

Not able to go on, Allie turned around and made her way back to the meeting tree. She sat and pulled her GPS from her backpack. She brought up the tracking map and followed where she had gone with Geneva to find the geocache, their return to the car, and the little side trip where she tried to follow Drake and Ingrid's path.

"I really need a map of this park," Allie said.

She exhaled, stood, and began her trek back to the parking lot. When she arrived there, she took a picture of the park sign, then got back into the car.

"Did you find them?" Geneva asked.

"Nope. I continued down the trail they did, but it turned into a waterfall with this rain. Were you able to call them?"

"Nope," Geneva said. "I can't get through to anyone. And before you ask, no one else has come through while you were gone."

"You're telling me that mountain climbing during a monsoon isn't on people's lists of fun things to do? I'm shocked!" Allie said with added snark in her voice. "Sorry. Can I have the keys?"

Allie turned around and Geneva passed her the car keys. Allie fired up the engine and turned the heat on high. Then she retrieved her handheld and compared the tracking map to the picture she'd taken with her phone.

"What are you doing?" Geneva asked.

"I'm trying to get a feel for these trails. I'm wondering if the one we were on would have circled back around. Oh, crap."

"What?"

"I cut off half of the sign. I have to go take another picture."

Allie got out of the car and walked back to the sign. There was a large puddle between her and the sign that she needed to give a wide berth to avoid, and when she did, she went way past the sign and noticed for the first time there was a plastic box attached to the rear of the original sign. She stepped up to the box, opened it up, and pulled out a sheet of paper.

"Son of a bitch," Allie said as she noticed what was on the paper.

Allie slid back into the driver's seat, huffed loudly, and slammed the door.

"What?" Geneva asked.

"Look what I found." Allie passed a copy of an updated trail map to Geneva.

"Where'd you get this from?"

"A box on the sign we all somehow overlooked. It looks recent, at least as of two months ago."

Allie studied the new map and compared it to the tracks on her handheld. "Yep. It would have taken seven kilometers, but that trail would have eventually looped around and met up with the branch Drake and Ingrid took."

"Seven kilometers? What's that in American?"

Allie thought for a second. "Four and a half, perhaps. I know a 5K run is just over three miles."

"Now what? Are you going back out there to take a four-mile walk in the rain?" Geneva asked.

"I don't see like there's another choice," Allie said. "And it would be more like nine miles, since I can't complete the loop with the trail blocked by water. I'd have to go back the way I came."

"That's too much. I should go with you," Geneva said.

Allie turned and looked Geneva in the eyes. "We just had a big fight about that. You should stay here, and you know it."

"Maybe we should go for help. Go back to town."

Allie considered it. "What time is it?"

"One-thirty."

"Okay. The average person can walk four miles an hour, right? That's over an hour there and an hour back, so, three hours tops and I can be back."

"That statistic, if I'm not mistaken, is for even terrain under sunny skies. And I heard it's only three miles an hour, not four."

"Okay, three miles an hour is nine miles in three hours. And I'll add another hour. Let's say that if I'm not back in four hours, then you drive the car to town and get help."

Geneva considered it. "Okay. If you're not back by six, I'll run for the calvary."

Allie nodded. "Good. Just remember that this isn't Boston, so don't drive a hundred down the mountain and try to avoid honking at everyone and everything you see."

Geneva chuckled. "Ha, ha. Hold on a second before you go."

Geneva bent over and retrieved her pack from under her ankle, and rummaged through it until she found a few things. "Here. I have a bottle of water and three protein bars. Take it all."

"You sure?"

"Yes, I'm sure. I'm not the one going to be hungry and

thirsty out there. And you might need something for Drake and Ingrid."

"Good point. I wish we had more. I've only got a bottle of water on me," Allie said. She took the items from Geneva and stuffed them in her pack. "We should have packed more food and water."

"Why would we? I think this was the only hard cache on the list and everything else was relatively close to a town where we could get food, water, and gelato anytime we wanted," Geneva said.

"You had to mention the gelato?" Allie said.

Geneva smiled. "You get moving, find our friends, and before you know it, we'll be back at the shop. Maybe I'll buy you a double scoop of something."

"Okay, I'm going to hold you to that," Allie said.

"Hey, you forgot this," Geneva said, holding out the map.

"That's your copy. If someone comes by, you can tell them what happened and where I went."

"Yellow trail?"

"Yep, that easy-peasy yellow trail anyone could do."

"Wait!" Geneva said. "What if someone comes and they don't speak English?"

Allie thought for a moment, then shrugged. "I don't know, Geneva. I'm sure you'll figure something out. If I don't leave now, I might never, so I'm going now."

Allie shut off the engine, dropped the key fob into the cup holder next to the driver's seat, and left the car. Outside in the rain, she donned the backpack and adjusted the straps for a better fit. She took a deep breath, then, for the third time that day, headed toward the trailhead.

A bolt of lightning flashed off to her side, followed shortly by a rumble of thunder.

"I should have picked up a different hobby, like painting watercolors or knitting scarves," Allie muttered as she stepped onto the trail.

# CHAPTER EIGHT

"Well, hello there," Drake said as Ingrid opened her bright blue eyes.

"Hello yourself. How are you doing?" Ingrid asked.

"Not too bad. I'm thirsty. I have a lump on the back of my head the size of a baseball, and I seem to be growing a tree from my stomach."

Ingrid nodded. "That about sums it up. And one of those three I can actually do something about."

Ingrid retrieved Drake's backpack, opened it up, and withdrew a bottle of water. She cracked the seal, then handed it to him.

"Thanks. How did I get here?" Drake asked. "Come to think of it, where is here? I don't remember seeing this cave during the hike."

"Well, I don't know exactly where we are. Do you remember anything about what happened?"

Drake gave his head half a shake. He winced and stopped. "No, I don't."

"Well, the short version of the story is, you thought it would be a good idea to keep going on the trail, and from what I saw, you snagged your foot on something. When you pulled it loose, you lost your balance and headed ass over teakettle down the mountain."

"You're kidding."

"If I were, we'd be in a nice bistro somewhere drinking coffee and eating whatever the Italian version of scones is," Ingrid gathered her backpack, found her own water within, and had a swallow. "Allie would probably tell us."

"Tell us what?"

"What the Italian version of a scone is," Ingrid said.

Drake thought for a moment. "I don't know what it could be. You're right, though. Allie would. She knows a remarkable amount of random trivia. How did you say we got here?"

Ingrid clambered to her feet and stretched her hands overhead and cracked her neck and back. Once she limbered up, she sat back down next to Drake.

"It was no big deal. Once you disappeared over the cliff, I made my way down the mountain, found you, and single-handedly carried you into this dark, damp cave."

"You? Carried me?" Drake asked. "Thank you. I take it I was in a bit of trouble?"

A grave expression passed over Ingrid's face. "Let's just say I expected to find you dead, or never find you at all. I suspect if you'd continued on another twenty feet, it would have been both."

"Thanks for finding me and for getting me to safety," Drake said.

Ingrid shook her head and frowned. "Neither one of us is safe quite yet. All I did was get us under shelter from the rain. We're a way off from the main trail, and I'm not sure if I can get back the way I came. And I know you wouldn't be able to do it with a branch sticking out of you."

"I'm sure I could yank it out and be fine," Drake said, lifting his shirt and looking at the protrusion.

"I'm equally sure that would be the last stupid thing you'd ever do. You know better than I do. It should stay where it is until you can get professional help."

"You're a professional," Drake said.

"I'm an English teacher. If you want to write an essay about it, then I'll be of help to you. Otherwise, let it go."

Drake grinned. "Got you."

Ingrid rolled her eyes. "Jerk."

"I'm tired," Drake said. "Really tired."

"I'll bet. I shouldn't have fallen asleep and let you doze off. You might have a concussion."

"First off, based purely on the lump on my head, it would surprise me if I don't have one. Second, I'm pretty sure experts debunked the whole don't go to sleep with a concussion thing."

"You sure about that?" Ingrid asked.

Drake shrugged. "Sixty percent."

Ingrid smiled. "Such confidence. I love that in a man."

"Sorry, I'm already taken."

"Yeah, me too. So, before you go off into dreamland, what are we going to do here?"

"I assume you already tried to call for help and couldn't reach anyone?"

"Correct. We have no service."

Drake took a drink of water as he pondered their situation further. "You sure we're off the trail?"

Ingrid nodded.

"How far? Can you tell?"

Ingrid retrieved her GPS from her pack and booted it up. "That geocache had parking coordinates, right? I should be able to tell how far we are from those. The only problem is, they'd be straight up the mountain. I don't know how far I traveled to find you, but most of it was downhill. I passed one deer trail somewhere above us, and then there's this one we're on now, but

I don't know where they lead, if anywhere."

"Would you guess we're a half mile off the main trail?" Drake asked.

"For sure. Probably more. Hold on, I've got no signal here in the cave. I'm going to step outside and see if I can get better reception."

Ingrid got to her feet and headed toward the cave's mouth.

"Hey, wait," Drake said. "Are you bleeding?"

Ingrid stopped and looked down at her leg. It was the first time she had stopped for a good look. She had shredded the pants in several strips, each at least six inches in length. The jeans contained dark ribbons of blood, but it didn't seem fresh.

"You should let me take a gander at that," Drake said.

"No, way, mister. There's no way I'm dropping my pants for you. I got us this far, so I'm sure I'll live. I'll be right back."

Ingrid stepped from the cave and found the largest open spot she could find. Eventually, the geocache list came up, and she selected the closest one and started to drill into the parking coordinates when the unit blinked rapidly several times and the screen grew dark.

"Shit," Ingrid said. She pressed the power button, but nothing happened. Standing in the rain, she flipped it over, opened the back, and dug out the batteries. Ingrid inspected them, saw nothing wrong, then shoved them back into place and buttoned the unit back up. Again, the power button failed to work, so she hit the unit several times, knowing full well that objects often responded to brute force. Dejected, she headed back to Drake.

"My GPS isn't working. Can I try yours?"

"My unit is your unit," Drake said. "Should be in my pack."

Ingrid went through his pack and found it. She looked at it once, then shook her head.

"What?" Drake asked.

Ingrid turned the unit around. The screen looked cracked,

and although it shouldn't happen, a chunk of the top corner was missing.

"And with my luck, the warranty period expired," Drake said.

"I guess it's back to the question of what we should do," Ingrid said.

"Well, experts say that if you get lost in the woods, you should stay put and wait for help to get to you," Drake said.

"True. But I wouldn't call this a normal woods situation. It's not like there's going to be a lot of hunters or hikers where we are."

"I think we have to try to walk out of here when the rain stops," Drake said. "It can't rain forever, can it?"

Ingrid smiled. "No more than forty days and nights at one time."

"I heard that somewhere once, too. Can you help me up?"

Ingrid stepped in front of Drake. With a grunt, helped him to his feet.

"Let me go," Drake said.

"Are you sure?"

Drake passed her a look, and Ingrid released him and backed away two feet. Drake took a step forward, then hesitated. Instead of moving forward, he stepped back again.

"Help me back down."

Ingrid did as she was told, and Drake rested his back against the cave wall.

"How did that feel?" Ingrid asked.

"Like someone had stabbed me with one of those wooden lances that knights jousted with. I think I could walk, but not far, and there's no way I can climb anywhere, other than into a bed."

"Okay," Ingrid said. "What's the plan?"

"Well, survival in the woods is usually about shelter, food, water, and fire," Drake said. "We're a quarter finished already, thanks to you."

"More if you count the water we have on us," Ingrid said. "How much do you have?"

Drake held out his half-filled bottle. "This much. You?"

Ingrid held hers up. It was three-quarters full.

"Okay. The first step of the plan is to put mine outside and let the rain fill it. See if there's a spot where you can use a palm leaf to funnel more water into the bottle."

"Palm leaf?" Ingrid asked.

"Wishful thinking. Find something that isn't poison ivy, oak, or sumac."

"Okay."

Ingrid grabbed his bottle and stepped outside. Off to the cave's side, opposite from the direction they'd come, she found a spot where the rain fell almost straight down at a steady rate. She looked up, following the source, and guessed it was a twist of fate that had the water dripping down through the trees as it did. She placed the bottle on the ground beneath the stream, and stacked rocks around the bottle so it wouldn't tip over. Ingrid watched the flow for a moment and estimated the bottle would fill to the brim within fifteen minutes if the rain kept up.

"What's next?" Ingrid asked as she stepped back into the cave.

"Food or fire. What do we have for food?" Drake said.

Drake dumped out his backpack. He had a chocolate bar and a pack of gum. Ingrid rooted through her pack and added two granola bars.

"Not much," Ingrid said.

"No matter. Water's the important thing. We can worry about food later. Now, what about fire?" Drake asked.

"Oh, I got that one handled," Ingrid said. "I'll be right back. I need to do a little exploring."

Ingrid dumped the contents from her backpack in a pile next to Drakes, then picked up his pack as well.

"You got your phone on you, or did you lose it?" Ingrid

asked.

Drake leaned over and pulled his phone from the front pocket of his jeans. "Fortunately, I was smart enough to tuck this away before I fell."

He handed the phone to Ingrid, and she took a look at it. Like his GPS, the phone was trash. The screen appeared shattered, and there was a hairline crack along the backside. Ingrid shook it and water dripped out of the charging port. She tossed it back to him.

"You're kind of hard on electronics, Drake."

Drake caught the phone one-handed, looked it over, and threw it on the pile of stuff.

"I'll be back in a minute," Ingrid said. She turned and walked farther into the cave.

Once she got away from the wide cave mouth, the light dropped from dark gray to black in an instant. Ingrid dug out her phone and turned on the flashlight function. A foot off to her left, she found a bunch of dry pine needles on the cave floor. She gathered them into a pile, then brushed them into a backpack. Near the needles, she scored big time and found a brittle branch at least eight feet long. She dragged the branch all the way back to Drake, asked him to break it into smaller pieces, and headed back into the cave again.

Ingrid took her time exploring the cave. Every piece of wood or kindling she could cram into the backpacks, she did. Needles, leaves, or branches. If she thought it would burn, she collected it. Whatever wouldn't fit into the bags, she carried back to Drake and built a pile.

Satisfied she'd collected enough for the moment, Ingrid went back to Drake, emptied her bags, and sorted her stash by type and size.

"What are you doing?" Drake asked.

"Magic. Sit tight, buddy."

Ingrid stepped into the rain, looked around, and started

throwing rocks into the cave, just inside the entrance. Since she was already out and getting wet, she checked Drake's bottle, found it full, and returned it to him.

"Here's some fresh water. Hopefully, you don't get any bugs," Ingrid said as she handed him the bottle. Drake looked at the contents, shook the bottle to see what debris was floating in it, and then set the bottle aside.

Ingrid gathered up the stones and formed them into a rough circle, approximately two feet across. Then she added a small pile of pine needles to the center of the pile, along with several twigs.

"You have a match on you?" Ingrid asked.

"What?"

Ingrid grinned. "Never mind. Throw me your handheld and that gum."

Drake brushed through the pile, located the items Ingrid wanted, and tossed them over to her.

"What are you up to?" Drake asked.

"I already told you that. It's magic."

Ingrid extracted a piece of gum from the pack and put the stick in her mouth. Then she carefully folded the wrapper lengthwise and folded it back over itself. She unfolded the wrapper, then carefully tore the wrapper into three thin strips. Then, working as deliberately as she could, Ingrid tore pieces away from the center of a strip until only a thin segment remained. She repeated the process with the other strips, and when she finished, she had three nearly identical strips that resembled little foil hourglasses.

Ingrid set the wrappers down, cracked open Drake's GPS, retrieved the AA batteries from inside, and tossed the rest of the broken unit away. Ingrid placed one of the batteries inside the fire ring, right next to the pile of needles.

"I hope this works," Ingrid said.

"What?" Drake asked.

Without answering, Ingrid grabbed one of the small strips

of gum wrapper, folded it over so the foil ends were on the inside, and depressed them around the positive and negative terminals of the battery.

"Ouch!" Ingrid said as a tiny spark erupted from the wrapper and lit the pine needles. Ingrid licked her forefinger and thumb, then quickly pulled the battery from the fire, and tossed it into the cave. It rolled for a foot and stopped right in front of Drake.

"You've got to be kidding me," Drake said. "That's amazing. Where did you learn to do that?"

Ingrid smiled as she fed the fire a few of the twigs and began to scatter them atop the building flames.

"All Danes are natural arsonists," she said. She caught Drake's shocked look and smiled. "Okay, strike that. When I was little, I spent a few years in the Girl Scouts. Can you come over and tend the fire?"

"Sure thing," Drake said. He had four feet of ground to cover, but rather than attempt to stand and walk, he got on his hands and knees and approached the fire that way. Ingrid moved the firewood pile, so it was closer to Drake. She rubbed her hands over the fire, enjoying the warmth.

"You know how to do this?" Ingrid asked.

"Yep," Drake said. "I have enough camping trips under my belt to give me the experience."

Ingrid nodded. "Okay. You keep an eye on the fire, and I'm going to see if I can find any more fuel. Since I don't know how long we'll be here, I want to gather as much as I can now."

"Good idea," Drake said. "And good luck."

Ingrid nodded, grabbed the empty backpacks, and headed back inside the cave.

She had a mental image of where she walked, so she didn't bother turning on the light until she was a good ten feet into the cave. Once again, she scoured the cave for fire materials, and finally, she reached the end of the cave where it came to a T junction.

Closer to the right wall, she turned right and immediately the walls closed in, the cave sides no farther than three feet apart from each other. She followed the path, but found it void of burnable material except for one three-foot-long stick. After fifteen feet, she came to a dead end and turned around.

Ingrid returned to the junction and continued straight. After four feet, the walls closed in on her, forcing Ingrid to turn sideways to fit in the corridor. She side-shuffled her way for twenty feet when the walls blew out again and Ingrid found herself in a large cavern.

She lifted her phone above her head, hoping to illuminate the area, but the darkness absorbed the light after six feet. Ingrid walked with the wall to her right, finding nothing until she spotted something that looked like a jacket. As she stepped closer, she realized the item was not a coat at all, but rather an old wool blanket. As she picked it up, the stiff fibers scratched against her arms, and by chance she looked at where the blanket had laid on the floor. There, on the floor, was a pile of stones laid out in the shape of an arrow.

Curious, Ingrid moved forward and another twenty-five feet later, she encountered a wall. Sitting on the floor before her were a couple of hand tools she didn't recognize. She picked them up and placed one in each back pocket. When she ran her light over the wall, she spotted something she didn't expect. Crudely cut into the wall was a bas-relief of an elephant.

"What in the world?" Ingrid asked to the empty room.

The sculpture showed the elephant in profile, and although some of the detail had worn away with time, the large body, rectangle legs, gigantic head, floppy ears, and tusks were unmistakably those of an elephant.

On either side of the elephant were two-foot-high curved tusks carved into the wall, covered in mosaic tiles, some of which were missing.

Ingrid couldn't help herself, so she ran her fingertips over the elephant, feeling the intricate detail. When she finished, her fingers drifted over to the tusk to her right. The tactile differences in the tile were striking. Some were polished smooth, like glass. Others seemed pitted and craggy, like stone. As Ingrid ran her fingers over one tile in particular, the cold sensation of its surface felt to her like a metal of some sort. Not intending to, she applied a little pressure, and the tile slipped from the sculpture and clattered when it hit the stone floor.

Ingrid looked around like security had caught her vandalizing an art museum, then bent and retrieved the piece she'd dropped. She attempted to place the piece where she'd knocked it from, but it dropped again. Ingrid caught it in midair and held it in her palm for a minute, thinking about what to do.

At last, she got an idea. From her mouth, she took the gum she'd been chewing on the entire time and placed it on the inside of the tile. Then she placed the tile where it belonged and pushed.

What Ingrid expected was that the gum would stick to the wall, holding the tile in place. Instead, Ingrid heard a loud click, and suddenly the elephant before her slid back into the wall, and off to the side, revealing a secret compartment.

Ingrid moved closer, brought the light up, and shined it in the hole.

# CHAPTER NINE

"I should have never agreed to the plan. We should have gone as a group. Together. Never, ever should have split up," Allie mumbled as she stepped down the initial stairs leading to the main trail. "Nothing good ever happens when the group splits up."

Allie reached the bottom stair, stopped, yawned, and moved on.

"We should all be in a nice, warm, dry museum somewhere. Looking at four-thousand-year-old art and listening to Drake whine about how he wants to leave. Or in a little cafe in some little town where they only speak Italian, eating pasta and drinking wine and telling stories until the rain lets up. But no. I'm out here in that rain, trudging around a mountainside, looking for my lost people."

Since she'd covered the same section of trail several times already, she recognized the area as she walked. Allie moved swiftly, aware of where to step, and less afraid that she'd make a misstep along the way. She still avoided the puddles where she could, but her mission had long drifted from worrying about remaining dry and clean. That train had blown well past the station.

"Nine miles. That's a long way, Allie," she said to herself. "Are you even ready for nine miles? In reality, probably not. Will your bad knee hold up for nine miles? Again, probably not. The smart thing to do would go back to the car, overcome your fear of the road, drive down the stupid mountain, and find a big St. Bernard, preferably carrying a little barrel of brandy. Let the dog find Drake and Ingrid. But today isn't about doing smart things, is it?"

The thunder rumbled in answer, and Allie glanced up toward the sky, although she couldn't see it. She thought perhaps the rain had lessened, but realized the section she currently sped-walked through contained a dense section of trees that prevented a good amount of rain from falling directly to the ground.

"Perhaps geocaching the Alps wasn't a good idea, after all. It's my fault we're here. Drake warned me about this, about going crazy with ideas, but I didn't listen. I could have written down a tropical beach location. Hawaii. That would have been a better idea. No, wait. That has jungles. And volcanoes. No. Not Hawaii."

Allie stopped for a second, realizing she'd been walking without bothering to track her surroundings. She turned around and glanced at the scenery behind her. Everything still looked familiar, so she restarted her walk. She plodded on in silence for several minutes, and at last she came to the downed tree where they all should have reunited hours prior. Rather than pull the paper map from her backpack and risk it getting drenched, she brought up the picture of it she'd taken with her phone. Up ahead a few yards, the trail split into the upper and lower sections, which looped around and returned to the junction.

She resized the image, making the section she was on bigger, and focused on that. With her finger, she traced the lower section she believed she'd already seen when she went to find her missing friends for the first time. She studied the curves and came to a conclusion.

"See, it's not as bad as you thought, Allie. Based on my estimate, I checked a good couple of kilometers already before that blockage. That's a third of the path I've covered."

Rejuvenated by her own pep talk, Allie headed for the upper trail. The trail followed a ridge and stayed relatively level for almost a mile. The trail appeared well groomed, free of rocks, limbs, and other debris, so even in the rain, Allie had no difficulties moving at a swift pace. After only ten minutes, she came to a section where the mountain overhung the trail. It was there where Allie and Geneva had initially waited undercover to see if the rain was going to let up.

Inside the cutout, someone had long ago carved out a five-foot length of rock, making a primitive seating area.

"Let's take a brief break," Allie announced as she slipped her backpack from her shoulders. She put the pack on the cutout and took a seat next to it. It actually wasn't a bad spot. With the falling rain going over the edge of the cutout, she got the impression that she was sitting inside a waterfall. Allie fought the urge to take off her shoes, and instead she massaged her left calf, and then her right. Once she'd relieved the tension in both legs, she withdrew a water bottle and had a mouthful of liquid, then stowed it back in her pack.

"You ready to go on, Allie?" she asked herself.

She thought for a moment, then answered. "No. Not really. I'd much prefer to stay here until it stops raining, and I dry up and get warm. I never thought much about the expression chilled to the bone, but I'm certainly feeling that way today."

Allie groaned as she pushed her way to her feet. "Time to go."

Allie returned the backpack to her shoulders, then stepped back into the rain. After another hundred yards, she recognized the fir tree where she and Geneva had turned around when the downpour started. The spruce was easy to recognize. It was right beside the trail, and someone had pruned away the bottom six feet of branches on the trail side. Allie walked on into the unknown.

She plodded for another quarter mile when she came to an area with several steps cut into the mountainside, supported by railroad ties, similar to the beginning of the trailhead. In this case, there appeared to be twice as many steps.

"Okay, let's take this one nice and easy, Allie. No missteps. No broken ankles."

Allie took the first step down and determined it was steep, but otherwise, wasn't too bad. The step slanted slightly, so the water ran to the edge, and from there, a channel carried the water down the slope. Allie stepped down the subsequent stairs with equal parts confidence and awareness, and she counted each step as she went.

"Lucky twenty-one," Allie said when she finally reached the bottom. "Whew, my legs are burning. I can't wait to go back up these."

Allie walked ten yards, found a downed tree stripped of bark bordering the trail and sat for a moment to rest. The tree was a long one, just over seven feet, and it tapered smaller in diameter toward Allie's left. As Allie leaned back to stretch, she looked to the left and then to the right. She returned to her normal sitting position, then leaned back again. There, about four feet to her right, sat an unnatural pile of rocks, otherwise known as a UPR. The UPR, a common way to hide a geocache in the woods, closely resembled its cousin, the UPS, or unnatural pile of sticks. The unnatural part came in because nature never stacked sticks or rocks in nice, symmetrical piles and then attempted to make them look natural. Only people did that.

Allie stood, moved over, sat back down, and began moving rocks. Sure enough, underneath the makeshift cairn was a plastic ammo box with a geocaching sticker on the side. Allie picked up the box, opened it, and squealed with delight. She removed an item from the ammo can, closed the box, and set it on the ground before her. Then she opened the package and donned the cheap florescent blue rain poncho she'd found in the geocache. She made sure the poncho cleared her backpack, then she put on the hood. Although the plastic was about the same quality Allie was familiar with from packing her own groceries at her local supermarket, it was good enough for the current situation.

Covered, Allie picked up the ammo can and checked to see if there was anything else useful inside. She found the paper log in a small plastic baggie, a string of plastic beads, two toy cars, one Euro coin, one American quarter, and a rock. The rock she took from the cache and dropped it at her feet. Then she closed up the ammo box, returned it to its spot, and covered it with the rocks.

"That was exciting. Score one for me," Allie said when she got back to her feet.

As Allie walked on, she discovered the lower loop seemed nowhere near as well-groomed as the upper trail. She found potholes galore to avoid, tree roots, and rocks to keep aware of, and her pace slowed considerably.

After an arduous twenty minutes of hiking, Allie came to a fork in the road. The marker attached to the tree nearby told Allie to stay on the upper trail where she was, but to her right, a well-used and pronounced deer trail branched down the mountainside. Allie retrieved her phone and checked the map. The yellow trail made a single loop, and where the group had divided earlier in the day was the only sanctioned trail. Allie shoved the phone back in her pocket and continued on the upper trail.

"I've got to be getting close by now. Ingrid! Drake!" Allie called out. She heard nothing back, so she kept walking. Fifteen minutes later, she came to a place she recognized. In front of her was a downed tree next to the trail, not unlike the several others she'd discovered on the trail. In front of this log stood a puddle of mud and water. Beyond the log was a short section of clear trail, and beyond that was the rushing water that blocked her path earlier.

Allie cupped her hands around her mouth and screamed. "Ingrid! Drake! Can you hear me? Drake! Ingrid!"

Allie stopped and waited, hearing nothing but the water near her and the sound of the rain hitting the earth.

Allie screamed their names repeatedly for five minutes, disheartened she hadn't heard a response. Although she wanted to cry, both for her missing friends, and from pure exhaustion, she didn't. Instead, Allie dropped her head and rubbed her temple. As she moved her hand, she looked down and spotted something unusual. She crouched and got as close to the ground as she could without sitting. There, she ran her fingertips over the shoe print in the mud.

Although only the back half of the print was visible, Allie still recognized it immediately. There was a stamp in the mud, and although it was backward, she read it easily.

"Converse All Star." Allie said. "From Ingrid's brand-new Chuck Taylors."

Allie's sense of relief was short-lived when it occurred to her that the front half of the footprint would have put Ingrid over the side.

"Oh, crap," Allie said.

She leaned as far forward over the side as she could without falling and looked for any evidence of Ingrid or Drake but spotted nothing. She backed away from the edge.

"Okay, Allie, think about this a minute. You didn't pass them on the trail, and there weren't many opportunities or a reason to go anywhere else but the trail."

Allie turned to her left and shoved the puzzle pieces into place.

"They came this way and got caught. Couldn't go back

because of the water, so tried to make it to this side of the trail to loop around when something happened here." Her eyes drifted from the log to the muddy path to the edge. "Oh, double crap."

Allie spent several minutes screaming the names of Drake and Ingrid into the void and got nothing in return for it.

"Okay, down it is, I guess," Allie said. She looked for a way down, starting with the spot where she found Ingrid's shoe print. Allie moved up the trail a few feet and found a place where she thought she could start down the mountain. She moved her foot off the trail, found the rock she wanted, hesitated for two long breaths, and pulled her foot back to the trail.

"Always wanting to do things the hard way," Allie said as she turned around and started jogging down the trail.

She almost ran past what she was looking for, and had to stop, turn herself around, and backtrack to where she found the deer trail that broke away from the main trail.

"I hope this leads somewhere," Allie said as she stepped onto the trail.

Unlike the main trail, the deer trail was, in a word, precarious. The trail ranged from between eight to twelve inches wide with prevalent rocks, tree roots, and the occasional section of underbrush that Allie needed to push through in order to move forward. All the while having to deal with slippery mud underfoot.

Still, Allie pressed on even though her speed had dropped to a leisurely walk, bordering on a stroll. In several places, the trail came to spots where nothing but a few inches of ground separated the mountain's wall and the drop off.

A half hour later, Allie came to another branch. She flipped a mental coin, and rather than veer right and farther down the mountain, she continued on straight. For the first fifty yards, the walk was easy going. The path widened and flattened out, and the tree cover lessened, so although that meant less protection from the rain, Allie could at least enjoy the sky for a little while as she walked.

Then, the trees closed back in, the mountain slope grew steep, and the trail narrowed to nothing wider than a shoe. Allie carried on for another twenty yards, stepped around a boulder, and came to a spot where the trail ended at a sheer drop that started twenty feet over her head, and fell another forty feet below her. Had Allie been an ibex or a chamois, she easily might have pressed on forward, but since she was neither animal, she needed to pivot on one foot to turn around.

Before she did, she paused.

"Ingrid? Drake?" Allie called out, hoping for an answer. She repeated her calls and waited for a few minutes. When she felt her feet cramp, she recognized it was time to move on.

Slowly, Allie made her way back to where the trail split, then turned left and stopped. The trail sloped down a good sixty degrees and it was at least a six-foot drop between where she stood and the bottom.

Allie noticed a sapling to her right, and bent it over, intending to use it as an anchor as she descended the short section of trail. The first two steps worked fine, but on the third, her foot slipped. As she struggled for purchase with her feet, the young branch separated from the tree. Allie landed on her backside and slid to the bottom of the short hill. Allie stopped when she reached the bottom, then got to her feet. Thin mud coated the entire back of her pants, and only the poncho had saved her top half from being the same. Allie didn't even bother to brush herself. Instead, she looked around until she found the next section of trail and moved forward.

"This isn't so bad," Allie noted as she trudged on.

The current trail was much wider, contained actual green space on both sides of the trail, and remained relatively flat. Five minutes later, Allie stopped.

"Seriously?" she asked.

Before her, blocking the way ahead, was a deadfall. The

giant spruce covered the entire width of the trail and had fallen in such a way that the massive root ball had wedged itself between two trees above the trail. The tree had then bent in on itself, and the top three feet had snapped in half, but remained connected to the tree by strips of bark. It dangled over the edge of the cliff like mistletoe. Between Allie and the opposite side of the trail were nine feet of thick fir branches, along with the debris it had brought along on its slide down the mountain.

Allie stepped back from the monster and analyzed the situation. She doubted she could go up and over, and she recognized that going the other way was out of the question, so it left her with no choice but picking her way right through the branches.

She stepped to the tree and moved the nearest branch. When she did, yellow and brown pine needles dropped from the branch and fell to the ground. As a test to see if the tree was old and brittle, Allie attempted to break off the branch. She couldn't. She moved out farther where the branch was narrower, and with some effort, snapped the branch.

"Clearly I'd need a chainsaw for this," Allie said under her breath. "Come on, girl, you can do this. Think of it as looking for a pine tree cache. You've found plenty of those before."

Instead of walking directly into the tree, Allie found a small gap in between boughs and stepped into that. There, she grabbed the branch in front of her, pulled it back until it was past her, then stepped through, letting the branch settle back in its original position. If the branch was pliable and small enough, Allie draped it over or under an adjacent branch to hold it in place. Regardless of the method, it made for slow going, and it took Allie ten minutes to gain eight feet of forward movement.

Once past the tree, Allie was able to gain speed again. Although the path grew narrower and the green space lessened, the terrain remained flat, and she hustled full speed ahead.

Allie stopped.

On the trail ahead, Allie saw a cave, and within the cave, she saw a flicker that implied a fire was burning. Her heart jumped, and she picked up the pace. She stopped in her tracks when she got to the mouth. A wide grin crossed her face when she saw Drake sitting on the floor, poking at the fire with a stick.

"Are you roasting chestnuts there, Duck-man?"

# CHAPTER TEN

Drake looked up, and his demeanor changed in a microsecond. "Allie!" He tried to get to his feet, lost his balance, and fell on his backside.

Allie rushed over and wrapped her arms around his neck. "Drake! I can't tell you how happy I am to see you."

"How did you know we were down here?" Drake asked.

"Are you kidding me? I'm three-quarters bloodhound," Allie said.

Drake's expression told Allie he wasn't buying it.

Allie stripped off the poncho and sat down cross-legged in front of the fire opposite Drake. She leaned forward, warming her hands.

"Okay, you got me. I spotted Ingrid's footprint in the mud, made a few general assumptions, ran into both good and bad luck and viola. Here I am. Speaking of whom, where is Ingrid? What happened to you guys?"

Drake threw a thumb over his shoulder. "She's back in the cave looking for stuff to burn. I suspect she's convinced we're never going to get out of here."

"She's safe, then?" Allie asked.

Drake nodded. "She saved me, Allie. I almost died out here, and she pulled me up the mountain and into this cave."

"No way," Allie said.

"Way."

"Tell me all about it," Allie said.

As Drake tended the fire, he spent several minutes giving Allie the story, at least, as much of it as he remembered.

"That's the worst story I've ever heard," Allie said when Drake finished.

"Ingrid would tell it much better. I think she was awake for more of this adventure than I was."

"How are you feeling? Anything broken?" Allie asked.

"No breaks, so far as I can tell. I've got a lump on my head, and this."

Drake lifted his shirt, exposing the protrusion.

"Holy cow, Drake, what did you do?" Allie asked.

Allie got to her feet and rushed to Drake's side, where she inspected his injury.

"What do you think, doc?" Drake asked after she checked his head and settled back down by the fire.

"Well, you're in need of an actual doctor. I don't imagine you have any internal bleeding, so I'm not even going to entertain the idea of ripping that wood out of your stomach. And as for your head, you'll need a scan for that. Thankfully, it was your head, so you couldn't have done too much damage."

Drake stuck his tongue out at Allie and laughed despite himself.

"Hey, Ingrid's injured, too. Her leg looks messed up, but she wouldn't let me check it out."

"Thanks for the heads up. She ventured into that cave, you said? To search for wood?"

Drake nodded. "Yeah. She's been gone a while now. I don't know what's up."

"I'd better go track her down. Can you wait here?"

Drake smiled. "I'm pretty sure I can handle that."

Allie grabbed her backpack and fished out a flashlight.

"You hungry?" Allie asked Drake.

"Do you have a T-bone steak in there? Medium-rare? Baked potato with the works, and a side of fried shrimp?" Drake asked.

"No, but I have a granola bar," Allie said, waving the bar in the air.

"I'll pretend," Drake said. "Thanks."

Allie tossed Drake the bar, who caught it in mid-air.

"We'll be back in a bit," Allie said.

Drake waved her off. "Take your time. I'm not going anywhere."

Allie clicked on the flashlight and stepped deeper into the cave.

Although Allie's flashlight was less than six inches in length, the LEDs illuminated a vast area within the cave. Nearby, she spotted a pile of longer branches she assumed was Ingrid's work and saw lots of tinder and fuel material that Ingrid had bypassed for some reason. Allie made it all the way to the cave's rear without finding Ingrid, but it wasn't long before Allie spotted the same corridors that Ingrid had. Like her friend, she tried the right one first and retraced her steps when she arrived at the dead end.

Once she backtracked and headed in the other direction, Allie quickly found the other room, and at the far wall, she spotted Ingrid.

When Ingrid saw her own shadow on the wall, she turned around and faced the light. She held up a hand to shield her eyes from the glare.

"Who's there?" Ingrid asked, her voice projecting a slight tremor of fear.

"The Ghost of Christmas Past," Allie said.

"What? Who?"

"Ingrid, it's me. Allie."

Allie dropped the light, so the beam struck the floor instead of her friend. She rushed across the room and caught Ingrid in a hug.

"I've gathered you've had a long day," Allie said.

Ingrid exhaled. "You could say that again."

"I also understand you're injured."

Ingrid waved it off. "It's nothing. Simply a tiny scrape."

"Maybe. I still want to glance at your leg when we get back to the sunlight. Speaking of which, why have you been gone for so long?"

"I found something. Let me have your flashlight."

Allie handed over the light without question, and Ingrid took it and turned back toward the wall.

"What are you doing?" Allie asked as Ingrid shined the light into the hole.

"Seeing what's in here," Ingrid answered. "I found this secret compartment, and I think there's something in here."

Ingrid set the flashlight on the edge of the compartment, stood on her tiptoes, and reached in as far as she could. Her arm disappeared past the elbow.

"I almost got it. I can feel it. It's just out of reach," Ingrid said. "Arrrghh!" she screamed. Ingrid went silent, her mouth opening and closing like a carp in a koi pond. Her eyelids fluttered, and her eyes rolled back in her head.

"Ingrid?" Allie said, stepping forward. She put her hand on Ingrid's shoulder. "What's going on? Ingrid?"

Ingrid's eyes focused on Allie's, and a wide grin spread across her face. "Gotcha."

Allie gave Ingrid's shoulder a push. "Not funny. Really. Not funny."

"Sure, it was. I've waited my entire life to do that to someone. I'm glad it was you."

"Would you quit messing around?" Allie said.

"Can you reach in there for me? My arm is like an inch too short," Ingrid said.

Allie stared at her without speaking.

"Seriously, Allie. It's an inch out of my reach. I can feel it, but I can't grab it."

Allie and Ingrid stood about the same height, but Allie's arms were a touch longer than Ingrid's.

Allie gave her a double take and switched positions with Ingrid. She put her arm in the hole and looked back at Ingrid.

"Don't think about it," Ingrid said.

Allie smiled. "Little old me? I would never. I got it."

Allie removed her arm from the chamber, and in her hand was an item, and she handed it to Ingrid.

"Anything else in there?" Ingrid asked.

"Nope, it's empty."

"Okay. Watch this." Ingrid located the proper tile on the tusk and pressed it. There was a clunk, a hiss, and the bas-relief pushed back into place.

"Is that an elephant?" Allie asked.

"Amazing, isn't it?"

"Sure is." Allie pulled her phone from her pocket and snapped pictures of the elephant and the tusks.

"Anything else to see in here?" Allie asked.

"Don't know. I didn't have a flashlight. You can look around if you like."

"Let's do it."

Allie took the flashlight and together, the women walked around the room. Allie focused the flashlight on the walls and floor, and soon they covered the entire area, finding nothing.

"Satisfied?" Allie asked.

"Yeah. I'll grab the blanket I found, and we'll head back to Drake."

Allie lit the way, and Ingrid picked up her treasure, and together, they headed back to the entrance. Near the fire, they found Drake lying on his side, softly snoring, the empty granola bar wrapper in his hand.

Ingrid covered him with her newly found blanket, then returned to Allie and embraced her in a bear hug.

"Did I tell you how happy I am to see you?" Ingrid asked.

"Not yet, but I'm ready." Allie wrapped her arms around Ingrid, and her hands moved down to Ingrid's back pockets. "What's this? You have something in your pocket, or are you happy to see me?"

"Oh, yeah." Ingrid broke away from the hug and stepped back. From her back pockets, she extracted the tools she'd found. In her left hand, she held a wood-handled trowel, the blade of which was crusted with rust, and looked like they salvaged it from the sea. In her right hand, she held a wood handle. Whatever was connected to the head had disappeared over time.

Allie took the tools and set them on the ground. "Can I take a look at that leg now?"

"It's not a big deal, just a little scrape," Ingrid argued.

Allie shook her head. "Don't argue. Just drop your pants and let me look."

"What about Drake?"

Allie looked over Ingrid's shoulder and noticed Drake hadn't moved an inch. "Drake is sleeping. Come on, let's get this over with."

Ingrid sighed but complied. She undid her jeans and gritted her teeth while she inhaled as she slowly lowered her pants. She turned so Allie could have access to her leg.

"Oh, man. You're lucky I consider scars are sexy because I expect you're going to have a couple."

"Is it bad?" Ingrid asked.

"You look like you were either dragged by a horse across Oklahoma or slid down a mountain in Switzerland. Why don't you lay down on your side and try to get comfortable? I'll be right back."

Ingrid looked around for a comfortable place to settle in, and while she did, Allie retrieved her poncho and laid it down on the ground and spread it out as much as she could.

"Here, lay your butt on this," Allie said.

Allie went and retrieved her backpack. From it, she pulled her water and a pair of white socks in a plastic sandwich baggie.

"What are you doing?" Ingrid asked.

"Lay still and try not to move."

Allie removed the socks from the bag and put one over her hand like a glove. She wet the sock with the water, then gently wiped away the dirt and dried blood from Ingrid's hip, careful not to reopen any wounds.

"Drake told me you saved him. I'd like to hear your side of the story," Allie said as she worked on Ingrid's leg.

"There's not much to tell. We were on the yellow trail when the rain came. Then got cut off by a flood, and when Drake tried to carry on, he slipped and toppled over the edge. I climbed down the mountain and found him, then got us into this cave."

Allie chuckled. "This is going to be an amazing story once you learn how to expand the details and add a little more drama."

"Ouch," Ingrid said as she flinched.

"Sorry. You've got a stone about the size of a dime embedded in your leg that I'm trying to get out."

Ingrid flinched again. "That hurts. Leave it in there. I'll tell people it's a piercing."

"Oh, hush. I've almost got it." Allie picked at the stone a third time, and finally it let go of Ingrid's leg and dropped onto the poncho. A small trickle of blood came from the site, so Allie applied pressure to stem its flow. With her other hand, she picked up the stone and placed it into Ingrid's palm. "Here. You can keep this as a souvenir."

Ingrid eyed the stone for a moment, then closed her hand around it. "Thanks. How's it looking back there?"

"Well, it doesn't seem as bad as it did before I started. I do think you'll need to see a doctor and get a better cleaning than I can give you with a sock. You might also take a course of antibiotics just to be safe. For now, though, I've done all I can do."

Ingrid rolled onto her butt, and Allie helped her up. While Ingrid got back into her pants, Allie cleaned up the area and stowed her supplies in her pack. When they finished, they both sat back near the fire.

"How did you find us?" Ingrid asked as she opened the protein bar Allie had given to her.

"I found an updated trail map. It turns out that the trail loops around just like we assumed it did. I found your footprint up top and pieced together what happened."

"So, you climbed down the mountain, too?"

Allie shook her head. "Didn't have to. Down the trail, the part you didn't get to yet, I found a deer trail that branched off down here. That's the way we're going to get back."

"Where was it?"

Allie pointed in the direction from where she'd come. "That way."

Ingrid shook her head. "I checked that way. There's a big pine blocking the road. Can't get through there."

"I got through. Took some effort, but I did it. After that, there are only a couple of spots that are a little difficult."

Ingrid took a bite, chewed, and swallowed. She washed it down with a drink of water before she spoke again. "What I meant was, I don't think Drake can get through there. He's got a bump on the noggin and a tree growing from his stomach."

"Yes, I saw them both."

"I can't get him through that tree by myself. Earlier, he had trouble talking and walking."

"He was talking pretty good when I got here. It's probably a result of the ding on his head. We'll let him rest for a bit. Together, I'm sure we can get him out of here," Allie said.

"Should we move him? Would that be the best thing to do

here? Why not just go back and get some help?" Ingrid asked.

Allie stayed quiet and considered the question for several minutes until she finally answered.

"I gave that a lot of thought, actually. Even when I hadn't found you guys yet. From here, it would take me about an hour and a half to get back to the parking lot. Then another, what, half an hour to the nearest town? Then time to get the professionals organized, then get back to the parking lot, then more time to get back here. I think it would be best to move him if we can and save the time."

"Couldn't you call for help from the parking lot?" Ingrid asked.

"Nope. No service up there, just as there's no service down here."

"Speaking of the parking lot, where's Geneva?"

Allie smiled. "She's the smartest of all of us. Geneva is back in our nice, warm car. Probably napping like a cat in the backseat."

"She didn't want to go with you?" Ingrid said. A frown fell across her face.

"No, it wasn't like that at all. She tried, but I wouldn't let her. She would never have made this trip on that ankle. Geneva made it as far as the trailhead before I noticed she was hurting, too. Her heart was in it, but her body wasn't. We have a plan, though. If I'm not back by six, she's heading down the mountain to call in the professionals."

Ingrid nodded and checked her phone. "It's three-thirty now. Think we can make it back in time?"

"I do. As long as we keep moving and keep breaks to a minimum."

Ingrid glanced over at Drake. He'd wrapped himself in the blanket and looked snug as a bug in a rug. "Is it worth the risk of moving him?"

"I think it's the best thing. We'll wake him up in a minute

and see how mobile he is. If he can walk and talk like a normal human, we'll go. If he can't, we'll stay and wait for Geneva and whatever the Swiss calvary is called."

Ingrid looked at Drake again and noticed his eyes were open. "I don't know about that plan. Maybe we should leave him here and trek out ourselves. We can say we never found him. I'm sure the bears will take care of him for us."

Allie looked confused, but it cleared when Ingrid gestured toward Drake with her chin. Allie nodded her understanding.

"But what will we tell poor Geneva?" Allie asked.

"Well, when we found that treasure last year, we put all the reward money in that account for us to split equally, right?"

"Yeah, so?"

"So even though I'm not good at math, I'm pretty certain a gazillion dollars split three ways is better than a split four ways," Ingrid teased.

Allie smiled. "Excellent point. And you know what? Geneva is young, pretty, smart, and talented. I'm sure she'd have no trouble finding another beau. In fact, I've always believed she was way out of Drake's league, anyway."

"I can hear you jerks, you know," Drake said as he rolled over and sat up.

The women laughed.

"We were kidding," Ingrid said. "Besides, who knows how hard it would be to get a bear in here?"

"Good point. Perhaps we should push him over the cliff instead," Allie said.

"Hey. No bears, and no cliffs," Drake argued. "I like the other plan. The one where we get going and get out of here."

"Are you sure? You looked awfully comfortable sleeping there," Allie said.

"That was only an illusion. This blanket is scratchy and smells like old cheese."

"Okay, Drake. We can go, but first I'm going to test your

mental acuity, and then walk you around a bit to see how you do. If you fail either of those tests, we're going to hunker down and wait for outside assistance. Deal?"

"Deal," Drake said without hesitation. "What do you want to do first?"

While Allie asked Drake a bunch of random questions, Ingrid sat still and stayed out of the way. Satisfied in the answers, Allie helped Drake to his feet. With a woman on each arm to prevent him from falling, Drake did several laps around the cave until he could walk on his own.

"Well, what's the verdict, doc?" Drake asked.

"I say we pack up, put out the fire, and hit the road," Allie said.

# CHAPTER ELEVEN

"Y'all ready to do this?" Allie asked.

Ingrid and Drake both nodded.

"I'll take the front. Drake, you stay on my tail, and Ingrid, you have the back. If anything happens, yell."

"Will do, captain," Ingrid said.

Allie looked around the cave one last time. They divided everything Ingrid had found and all the items they had brought with them among the three backpacks.

"By the way, you look adorable, Drake," Allie teased.

To protect his head and stomach, Allie had given the poncho to him.

"I agree," Ingrid said. "You look like a radioactive blueberry."

"I still say you guys are jerks. Can we get on with this already?"

The three got in line and stepped out from the cave and started down the trail.

"I think the rain has let up some," Ingrid said. "It's less of a tropical downpour, and more of a spring shower."

"I think you're right," Allie said. "Perhaps this day is looking up after all."

Allie kept a steady pace and looked back after every fourth step she took. When she determined Drake and Ingrid had no trouble keeping up with her, she changed to looking back every eight steps.

The fresh rain mixed with the pine and produced a scent that permeated the area, and Allie breathed in the moist air with equal parts enjoyment and gratitude.

"Are you doing okay back there, Drake?" Allie asked over her shoulder.

"I am. You can even pick up the pace a little if you prefer," he answered.

"I prefer not to, but thank you, anyway."

Allie stepped around a large puddle and carried on for another fifty yards until they came to the downed tree. She waited for the others to catch up to her.

"The path continues on the other side of this tree. I got here by pushing my way through it. We'll need to take this slow. There are plenty of places to get caught up here."

Drake studied the large obstacle. "You know I hate pine tree geocaches, right?"

Allie smiled. "This is better. There's nothing to find except the trail, and that's straight on ahead. Besides, this tree is dead, so other than the annoying feeling of getting pine needles down the back of your shirt, this should be easy."

"You wouldn't happen to have a saw in your pack, would you?" Drake asked.

"Sorry. I left my saw at the hotel. I wasn't planning on doing any forestry today. Everyone ready?"

Hearing no objections, Allie stepped up to the giant, trying to remember the path she'd taken through the thing. She picked one of the large branches at waist height and pulled it toward them as far as the branch would bend, hoping it would break off.

She detected no snap and determined she wouldn't get lucky with it after all.

"Ingrid, can you step in front of this and hold it until we're through?"

Ingrid nodded and walked around Allie and stood in front of the bough. "Okay, let it go, I got it."

Allie slowly released her grip, and the branch, wanting to spring back into place, caught on Ingrid's hip and stopped.

"Got it," Ingrid said. "It's pulling me, and I don't know how long I can hold it, so don't dawdle."

Allie stepped into the tree and grabbed the next branch in her way. She pulled and bent it back as far as she could, and as she was determining what to do with it, she heard a crack. She looked down at the bough and saw it splintered in half, although it remained attached to the trunk. Allie bent it back the opposite way, hoping to break it off completely, but it didn't. Instead, she pulled it back again, and tucked it behind another bough as if she were tucking a stray strand of hair behind her ear.

The next branch was only two feet off the ground, so Allie simply stepped over it, and as simple as that, she made it to the trunk. There, she stopped, wondering how she'd made it past it the first time she'd come through. The trunk was mere inches over three feet in diameter and leaned against a cliff wall the same way people often leaned against trees.

"Under, I must have gone under," Allie mumbled.

"What?" Drake asked.

"Only talking to myself. Hold on there."

"Not too long, Allie. This is getting heavy," Ingrid said. She shifted her body to regain her footing and stood still.

Allie spotted a broken branch, then it came to her, and suddenly she remembered. She'd squatted and duck-walked her way under the trunk close to the cliff wall.

"You think you can squat, Drake?"

Drake shrugged and tried it. He only got halfway down

when the color drained from his face, and he grabbed his stomach. He stopped and stood as straight as he could.

"That's what I was afraid of. Okay. New plan," Allie said.

Allie got to work, snapping off the smaller branches from the trunk in the space between the path and the wall.

"Here. Toss these," she said when she got a handful and passed them to Drake. Drake backed out from the tree and threw the branches over the cliff and headed back for a second round.

Satisfied she had removed all the impediments she could, Allie crouched and made her way under the tree. There, she removed what smaller branches she could from the other side and managed to push one of the larger boughs out of her way and secure it between two nearby branches. She nodded and returned to Drake.

"Come on in here, Ingrid," Allie said.

"All right," Ingrid said as she slowly walked toward her friends, careful not to let the branch she held snap fiercely back into place. As she joined the others, there was just enough room for the three of them, although Allie had to slump over slightly, and a nearby branch jabbed Ingrid in the ribs.

"Can you get the blanket?" Allie asked Ingrid.

"Drake has it."

Drake faced Allie, and Ingrid raised the poncho to get access to his backpack. The blanket didn't completely fit in the backpack, so it took no effort to find and remove it. When it was in hand, she passed it over to Allie.

"Okay, here's the plan. We're going to lay this on the ground, then you lay on it on your back and we'll pull you under the tree."

"That's the plan?" Drake asked.

Allie nodded. "The best one I can come up with." She folded the blanket in half the long way, then placed it on the ground. "Hop on. Put your head on the end closest to me."

To Drake's credit, he complied without a word.

"Ingrid, come with me and help me pull him through," Allie said. Once she finished, she made her way to the opposite side and waited for Ingrid to join her.

When Ingrid got to the other side, the women got on their hands and knees, hip to hip. They reached under the tree trunk, and each took a corner of the blanket.

"You ready?" Allie asked.

"I think so. Although it's still not too late to leave him."

"I can still hear you," Drake said.

"Okay. Count of three."

Allie gave the countdown, and with matching grunts, the women pulled on the blanket and Drake slid six inches toward them. They redoubled their efforts, yanked again, and Drake's head cleared the tree.

"Hi," he said. He smiled. "I kind of like this. Could you drag me the rest of the way back?"

"Okay, if I can knock you unconscious first," Allie answered.

She did another countdown, and on the third pull, Drake was clear of the tree up to his waist.

"You think you can sit up? We're running short of room in here," Allie said.

"You should have built a bigger fort," Drake answered as he sat up.

Rather than tug on the blanket again, Allie and Ingrid each took one of Drake's arms and pulled him backwards, free of the tree.

"Sit right there for a second," Allie said. "Ingrid, let's get you the rest of the way out of here."

Ingrid turned around and did a quick assessment. She stepped to her left, bent over slightly, and easily stepped around a branch, then pushed her way through the last one and held the branch still while she waited for the others.

Allie helped Drake to his feet, and Drake followed the path

Ingrid had taken. Allie grabbed the blanket, and within a few seconds, joined her friends. Once everyone was out, Ingrid stepped away from the branch, and it snapped back into place, showering the area with raindrops and pine needles.

"Well, that was fun," Drake said. "Where to next?"

Allie pointed up the trail. "That way. Should be relatively easy from here. You're in front, Ingrid, head on out."

Allie waited as Ingrid and Drake lined up and began hiking the trail. She recognized both were hurting to some degree. Ingrid was favoring her bad leg, and Drake was shuffling more than walking. But to their credit, neither of them uttered a word of complaint.

They marched in silence for several minutes until Ingrid stopped.

"Um. Yeah," she said.

"I forgot about this," Allie said. She stepped next to Ingrid and looked up at the short section of the trail that she'd slid down earlier in the day.

Allie stepped forward, dug her feet in, and attempted to scramble up the short hill, but her foot slipped from beneath her the second she put her full weight on it. She tried a second time and failed.

"It's not that high. We could probably boost you up, and you could grab on to that tree right there," Drake said.

"Then how would you get up there?" Allie asked.

"Ingrid would give me a boost," Drake said.

Allie looked at Ingrid, who rolled her eyes and shook her head.

"That's not happening," Ingrid said.

Allie stepped back to better assess the situation. To her right, there was a sheer wall that rose past the height of where the trail picked up again. To her left stood several boulders, each the size of their Fiat that were lined up like marbles. The top of the one closest to the crest of the hill was just a few inches taller than the upper part of the trail.

Allie pointed. "What if we got on those boulders there? We could go from one to another until we got to the trail."

"What's on the far side of the boulders?" Drake asked.

Ingrid stepped down the trail a few yards until she could see past the last boulder in line. "Looks like a straight fall down to the next outcropping of trees."

"How far is the fall?" Drake asked.

Ingrid shrugged. "I don't know. Thirty feet, maybe forty. Certainly, far enough that it would hurt if you hit the bottom."

"And then there's how we'd actually get up there," Drake said. "We have the same problem getting to the boulder top as we do getting up to the trail."

"Okay, okay," Allie said, conceding. "Poor plan."

"I got one. Give me a boost up," Ingrid said.

Without asking, Allie put her back to the slope, interlaced her fingers, and crouched. Ingrid stepped into Allie's hands, and Allie lifted her.

"A little more. I can't quite reach," Ingrid said.

"You're getting heavy," Allie huffed.

Drake stepped over and put his hands under Ingrid's flailing free foot and pushed. When Ingrid's weight shifted to the leg Drake was supporting, Allie spun around and pushed up on Ingrid's other foot. Together, Allie and Drake had enough strength to propel Ingrid to the upper trail.

"I made it!" Ingrid squealed with delight. "Toss your backpacks up here."

Allie and Drake removed their backpacks and tossed them up to Ingrid, who caught them and set them on the ground. Ingrid rummaged through them quickly, removing the blanket and anything else she deemed too bulky. She went to work on the shoulder straps next. Ingrid unbuckled the straps on her backpack and threaded one of the straps through an arm of Drake's, then attached the opposite strap to Allie's.

"Ta-dah," Ingrid said. She held up the interlaced backpacks that now resembled a rope ladder. "You can climb up this."

"You're not going to be able to pull us up," Drake said.

"Don't need to." Ingrid turned to the sapling Allie had busted in half earlier. She bent the sapling as far down as she could, then looped one of the backpack arms over the top. Ingrid worked on threading the flexible branches through until the backpack was on the ground. She flipped the end backpack over the hill, and the three dangled down and stopped just above knee height.

"No way that holds," Drake said.

"Come on, Mr. Negative, get on up there and give it a try," Allie said. She grabbed the bottom backpack and steadied it.

Drake stepped forward and put his foot on one of the shoulder straps. He put his full weight into it, and although the whole thing stretched, it held. Drake took the next step and grew more confident as he moved on to the next step. Within a minute, he joined Ingrid at the top.

"I told you this would hold," Drake said. "You think we should leave her here?"

Ingrid laughed, but Allie didn't think it was funny.

"I can hear you, you know," Allie said in her best imitation of Drake as she put her foot into the strap and began her climb.

Once she climbed to the top, they worked backward to remove the backpacks from the tree, separate the backpacks, and put everything back in order.

"That's the hardest part of this trail," Allie said.

"That's what you said about the tree," Ingrid said.

Ingrid took point, pushed on, and kept the party moving. After walking for several minutes, Ingrid stopped and groaned.

"You've got to be kidding me," Ingrid said, staring at the dozen stairs before them. "And if you dare say this is the hardest part of the trail, we're not stopping for gelato on the way back."

Drake moved to the nearby log and sat without saying

anything, and Allie sat down to his left.

"Are you hanging in there?" she asked.

"Honestly, I don't know how much farther I can go," he said.

Allie gently patted his knee. "We're almost out of here. We only need to go up these stairs to get to the upper trail, then it's a quarter mile to the trailhead. You can make it."

Drake nodded. "Can I at least rest a bit?"

"Sure thing."

Ingrid, seeing the other sit, took a spot next to Drake.

"I sure wish this rain would end," Ingrid said.

"I think it will soon. There's a break in the clouds and a little blue sky," Allie said.

"Where?" Drake asked.

Allie pointed to a break in the trees off to their right. It wasn't a large spot of blue, just enough to hint that the warm sun might still be up in the sky somewhere.

Ingrid sighed. "And to think we went through all this trouble and never found the geocache we came all the way out here for."

Allie smiled. "I don't know about that. Behind you, about a foot to your right, you'll find an ammo can under a pile of rocks."

"Ha. Ha. Now you're just being mean," Ingrid said.

Allie shrugged. "Okay. Don't get it then. I will after I sit for another minute."

"I don't think she's kidding, Ingrid," Drake said.

Ingrid leaned back and noticed there was indeed a pile of rocks next to the log. She undid the pile, exposing the ammo can beneath. She opened it and pulled out the plastic baggie holding the paper log.

"How did you know this was here?" Ingrid asked as she opened the baggie and fished out the log with her little finger.

"I found it by accident, just resting here on this log, like we're doing now."

Ingrid opened the front pocket of her backpack and extracted a black gel pen, attached her name to the log, and passed it to Drake. Drake signed and passed it to Allie, and Allie added her name and sent everything back to Ingrid.

Once Ingrid had everything back in order, she returned it to its hiding place.

"You ready to go, Drake?" Allie asked.

"Give me another minute, will you?"

"Sure, take all the time you need."

Allie got up and moved over to Ingrid's right, sat down, and took her hand.

"How are you holding up?" Allie asked.

Ingrid brushed a strand of wet hair away from her eyes. "I've had better days. I need a long, hot bath. And some food, and a nap. Perhaps all at the same time."

"Me too. As soon as we get Drake to a hospital and get that leg of yours looked at, we'll get those other needs of yours worked out."

"Great. Oh, and some gelato," Ingrid said. "That's for you."

"You said the magic word. Let's get a move on."

Allie turned to Drake. "You ready? Drake?"

Drake's eyes were closed, and he didn't move. Allie feared the worst, but then his chest hitched, and he took a deep breath. Allie gently shook Drake's shoulder and his eyes opened.

"Come on, tough guy. Your girlfriend is waiting for you."

Drake nodded and accepted Allie's help to his feet. He lurched forward to the bottom stair, then with notable effort put his left foot on it. With Allie's help and a loud grunt, he made it up one step. They repeated the process almost a dozen times until, at last, they climbed the final stair.

While Allie waited for Ingrid to ascend the steps, Drake lurched on ahead.

"He's not looking so good," Ingrid said. She accepted Allie's hand for the boost up to the last step.

Allie turned around and watched Drake for a few seconds. "We need to get him medical attention as soon as possible. Let's go help him along."

Allie and Ingrid jogged ahead, and although the trail didn't comfortably accommodate three people walking side by side, each woman took one of Drake's arms over their shoulder, and together, they powered down the trail.

When they reached the final stairs, Ingrid supported Drake from behind while Allie pulled him up the final steps. Finally, back at the trailhead, the three looked out across the parking lot to see the Fiat pulling away.

"I guess we missed our ride," Ingrid said.

Drake's knees buckled, and he dropped to the ground, pulling Allie with him. Ingrid leaned down to help the others up, and no one saw the Fiat's brake lights illuminate bright red against the dreary day.

## CHAPTER TWELVE

Allie tried to read an old John Grisham novel that she had owned forever. It had stood in her bookcase in her living room, along with a hundred other books on her pile of books to be read that she never seemed to get to. She had tackled the first few chapters on the plane ride over and vowed to finish it by the time she touched down back in America. Allie's eyes darted from the page to the door, and she lost her place again. Frustrated, she turned back exactly one page to where the chapter began, shoved a dollar bill there to mark her place, and set the book in the empty chair next to her.

Instead of the book, she picked up a magazine on the table next to her and began to page through it. Since it was in Italian, she couldn't read the words, and since worry distracted her, she barely noticed the images as she flipped the pages.

Allie heard someone coming, and she looked toward the door just in time to watch an orderly rolling a wheelchair into the room. Ingrid sat in the seat, and when she saw Allie, her face lit up and she giggled and waved. As soon as the nurse parked the chair and applied the brakes, Allie and Ingrid both stood and embraced.

"Hey, you." Allie said. "How are you doing?"

"Much better. You smell so good," Ingrid said as she broke the hug. "And thanks for the clothes."

"You're welcome. When we got here, the hospital staff wasn't all that happy with me tracking mud everywhere, so they strongly encouraged me to clean up. And I figured everyone needed a change of clothes, so I brought extra sets in for everyone from the hotel. How's the leg?"

"Feels fine, but that might be the pain medication they gave me before they cleaned me out and dressed the leg. They said I should have only a couple of small scars, but I had no major damage," Ingrid said. "And you were right about the antibiotics. Those are waiting for me at the pharmacy."

Allie moved the novel from the chair to the table, and Ingrid took the seat next to Allie.

"Have you gotten any news about the others yet?" Ingrid asked.

"Nope. You're the first. Drake needed surgery, and I think Geneva should be out any time now."

Ingrid yawned and reached for the ceiling with both of her arms.

"Tired, sweetie?" Allie asked.

"I think it's a combination of the drugs they gave me and coming off the adrenaline high. I'm hungry, too. What time is it?"

Allie activated her phone that sat on the table right next to her novel. "A little after nine. Should we go get something to eat?"

Ingrid shook her head. "No. I can hold out for a while. Let's wait for the others."

"Geneva's back," Allie said.

Ingrid turned to the door in time to see the same orderly that brought her out wheeling out Geneva. Geneva had a white plastic bag in her lap, and a cane in her hand. Like Ingrid, Geneva looked tired and ready for the day to end. The orderly rolled the wheelchair to the spot next to Ingrid and helped Geneva from the wheelchair and into the seat.

"You're still waiting for one more?" the orderly asked Allie.

"Yes. Drake Decker. The last update I received; he was still in surgery."

"I will go check on him for you," the orderly said.

"Thank you," Allie said.

Before the orderly left, she glanced at Ingrid and at Geneva. A smile crossed her Roman face. "It must be dangerous to be your friend."

Allie laughed. "Only when they don't feed me."

The orderly smiled, removed the brakes from the chair, and left the waiting room.

"What's your story, Geneva?" Ingrid asked.

Geneva placed her plastic bag next to the identical one Ingrid had on the floor and shifted in her seat to get comfortable. "There's not much to tell. Had an x-ray and found nothing was broken. From what I understand from the doctor, it's not even a sprain, more like a strain. I should be fine in a day or two."

"What's with the cane?" Allie asked.

"Simply a precaution. I insisted I didn't really need it, but they gave it to me, anyway. They suggest I use it for a couple of days if I refuse to sit in the hotel room the entire time I'm on vacation."

Ingrid smiled. "That's probably a wise choice. Unless you'd like to stay at the hotel while the rest of us are out having fun."

Geneva swatted Ingrid's leg. "No way. I didn't fly halfway around the world to sit in the room."

"We should take it easy for a few days." Allie said. "No more mountain climbing for the rest of this trip."

"Did either of you eat?" Geneva asked. "I could go for some pasta. What are those little pillow things called we had last night?"

"Gnocchi?" Ingrid offered.

"That's the one. I liked those. Let's get some once Drake comes out."

"Excellent idea," Allie said.

"You really think we should go to a restaurant looking like we do?" Ingrid asked.

"There's nothing wrong with the way you look," Allie said.

Allie turned her head and looked initially into Ingrid's eyes, then she expanded her view and saw what Ingrid was talking about. Ingrid's hair, normally a shade of blond so light it was almost white, had streaks of mud in it, and although Ingrid had done her best to wash up when she changed into fresh clothes, there was a smudge of mud behind her left ear, and a bit of grit beneath her right eye.

"Hold still," Allie said. She licked her thumb and wiped away the dirt from Ingrid's face. "There. You're good to go."

"What about her?" Ingrid asked, pointing a thumb in Geneva's direction.

Allie leaned over so she could get a better view of her friend. Geneva had escaped the mud tumbles that everyone else had taken, but not the downpour, so her short brown hair stuck out like hedgehog fur and was in need of dire attention from a brush.

"Hey, Geneva, you look great, too."

Geneva opened her mouth to protest, then closed it when the orderly entered the room.

"Your friend is out of surgery and recovery and moved to a room. If you follow me, I'll take you to him," the orderly said.

The three friends rose as one. Allie collected her phone and book from the table and then grabbed the three white plastic bags at their feet. Together, they followed the orderly to the elevator, up to the fifth floor, and down the corridor.

"General visiting hours are over at ten," the orderly said as she turned and left the area.

"Go on in," Allie said to Geneva, who was standing closest

to the door.

Geneva stepped over the threshold, followed by Allie and Ingrid.

Drake was sitting propped up in bed when the women entered. "Hi!" he said with equal parts excitement and fatigue. He wore a white and blue hospital gown, and an I.V. line stretched from his left arm to a machine next to the bed. On the machine hung two bags of medication.

Geneva headed over and gave Drake an extended kiss.

"What's that for?" Drake asked.

"Surviving," Geneva said.

"Then you need to kiss those two, too. I wouldn't be here without them."

Geneva turned and gave air kisses to Ingrid and Allie, then swung back around. "What's your prognosis?"

Before Drake could answer, Allie interrupted the couple as she lugged a chair from the room's corner to Drake's bedside. She nodded, and Geneva took the seat, still holding Drake's hand.

"I'm actually pretty well off for someone who fell off a mountain. Surprisingly, I don't have a concussion, just a big goose egg. And they took the tree out of my stomach. According to the surgeon, it didn't pierce any organs, so I got lucky there."

"What's with the drugs?" Geneva asked.

"A course of antibiotics, and a painkiller if I need one."

"When are you going to get out of here?" Ingrid asked.

"Probably tomorrow, unless my head gets wonky, or I have any post-surgical complications, which should be rare."

"Is there anything I can do for you?" Geneva asked.

"No darling, I'm fine. Although I don't think it was worth all this to find one cache."

A look of confusion crossed Geneva's face like an eclipse. "Wait, what? You found that cache?"

"No one told you?" Drake said. "Allie found it on the way to rescue us."

Geneva turned to Allie, a flash of anger in her eyes. "Our loved ones, lost and in danger out in the forest, and you stopped to find a geocache while looking for them?"

Allie waved her hands in front of her like she was trying to ward off a swarm of flies. "No, no. It wasn't like that at all. I found it on accident when I stopped for a rest. Tell her."

Allie looked from Drake to Ingrid, and back to Geneva.

Ingrid broke the tension with a laugh. "It's true. There was a log next to the trail, and the cache was behind the log. We practically sat on it when Drake needed to take a break. Since I was sitting right on top of it, I grabbed it and passed the log around. Sorry you can't get credit for it."

"Why not?" Geneva asked, her voice rising.

"You didn't sign the log. You know the rules, no sign, no find."

It was Geneva's turn to glance from Ingrid to Allie, trying to determine if they were serious. When she looked at Drake, she saw him trying to keep a chortle to himself. Finally, he broke.

"I wrote your name on the log," Drake said. "Even though technically it broke the rules, but we'll all consider it extenuating circumstances."

Geneva threw her arms in the air. "Not funny, you three. What am I supposed to do with you?"

"I know what you can do for me," Drake said.

Geneva turned to him and saw a sly smile on his face. "Drake. You're injured and have visitors. This is neither the time nor the place."

"No, not that," Drake protested. "Well, yes, that, but not now. Would you three be okay with leaving? I've had a really long day and I feel myself falling asleep."

"Are you sure? I can stay with you tonight," Geneva said.

"No. You can go. You have your own injury to tend to. I'll be fine here."

"Okay, honey. If you need anything, just call." Geneva

stood, leaned over, and gave Drake a soft kiss. She squeezed his hand, then stepped away from the bed.

Allie held up a plastic bag. "I brought you a change of clothes. I'll put them in the closet over here." Allie unpacked the clothes into the closet, then folded the bag and put it on a shelf. "Get good rest, Drake. I'll see you tomorrow."

"Thanks, Allie. I appreciate it. Hey, Ingrid?"

Ingrid stepped to Drake's bedside, and when she got there, he reached out for her hand.

"I owe you everything, Ingrid. I wouldn't be here if it weren't for you. Because of that, I owe you a debt I'll never be able to repay."

Ingrid smiled, then leaned over and kissed Drake's forehead. "Take good care of yourself, and good care of Geneva. That will be payment enough."

The pair extended the moment in silence, then Ingrid squeezed Drake's hand. "Go to sleep. We'll see you tomorrow."

Drake nodded and turned off his overhead light while Ingrid and Allie stepped from his room.

"I'm glad he'll be okay," Ingrid said.

Allie put her arm around Ingrid's shoulders. "Me too. What do you say we find some gnocchi for Geneva?"

An hour later, the three women sat around a table at a busy restaurant a block from the hotel. Ingrid and Geneva shared a bottle of wine between them while Allie sipped a glass of water.

"Here's to finally getting to eat," Geneva said as she raised her glass and touched it to the rims of the glasses of the two friends.

"I'll toast to that. You can't grasp how famished I am," Ingrid said. "I hope this place has good food."
Allie felt her stomach rumble. "At this rate, I'll take any food."

Like magic, a server appeared wearing black linen pants and a royal blue shirt with the restaurant's name embroidered above the pocket.

"*Buonasera,* ladies. Italian or English?" he asked.

"English, please," Allie said.

"Perfect. My name is Lorenzo. I see you're already situated on drinks. Do you know what you'd like to eat?"

Geneva handed Lorenzo her menu. "I'm going to have the potato gnocchi."

"Excellent," Lorenzo said as he took the menu. "What type of sauce would you like with that? I would recommend the pesto, tomato, or we have a nice sage butter sauce tonight."

Geneva thought for a moment. "I'll go with the butter sauce. Oh, and a salad, please."

"Excellent."

"I'll have the exact same thing," Ingrid said as she handed Allie her menu.

"Make it three," Allie said, handing the menus to Lorenzo.

"Perfect. Makes it easy for me. I'll return shortly."

"With Drake out of commission for the day, what should we do tomorrow?" Ingrid asked. "Geocaching as planned? Visit a museum or two? A spa day?"

Lorenzo stopped by the table and dropped off two small bottles. "For your salads. Olive oil and balsamic vinegar," he explained, then disappeared.

"A spa day sounds fantastic," Geneva said. "Manicure. Pedicure. Perhaps a mud mask."

Ingrid was in the middle of a drink when she started shaking her head, almost spilling her wine. "Uh, no. No mud. I've had enough of mud for this trip."

The women enjoyed a quick laugh, and as they finished, Lorenzo returned with the salads and meals. Starved, they quickly dove into their food.

Geneva took one bite of her gnocchi, chewed, swallowed, and picked up another tender potato pillow. "This is exquisite. I think it's even better than the ones we had last night."

"They are delicious," Ingrid said. "You know what would

go real good with this sauce?"

"Bread?" Lorenzo asked as he swung by the table and dropped off a basket of Italian bread. "Careful, it's just out of the over and still hot."

"No way," Geneva said. She reached into the basket, then withdrew her fingers quickly. "Oh, yes, it is." Using her fork, she extracted a slice, then blew on it until it cooled a bit. She took the slice between her fingers and dipped it into the butter sauce. Geneva took a bite and slowly savored the taste. "Hello, heaven. I think I'm in love."

Ingrid and Allie extracted slices themselves and copied Geneva's process. Casual conversation ground to a halt as the friends devoured their meals. Over the next half an hour, the only sounds at the table were the clinking of silverware on plates. Finally, all three of the women set their plates aside.

"So, back to tomorrow's plan," Geneva said.

"I'd be interested in finding out what this is. Maybe a trip to a library or something?" Allie said.

"What?"

Allie held up her phone and showed the others the picture. "The thing you found in the cave. When you were in the shower before, I cleaned out our backpacks and found it. This writing was on parchment."

"I just thought it was some animal hide. I didn't even bother to check," Ingrid said.

Allie finished her water and set the empty glass on the table. "I don't know what you found, but it must be something special if they hid it like they did." Allie zoomed in and held out the phone for all to see. "Look. It has what appears to be Egyptian writing on it."

"Pardon my looking over your shoulder, but that's not Egyptian. It's Punic," Lorenzo said as he topped off Allie's water.

"Punic? Never heard of it." Ingrid said. "Looks like hieroglyphics to me."

"Punic is an offshoot of the Phoenician language. When I'm not waiting tables, I'm a student of ancient history in Rome. I specialize in ancient Carthage, but since it was a Phoenician settlement, I'm familiar with the culture overall."

"Can you translate this? Tell us what it means?"

"Do you mind?" Lorenzo asked, pointing at her phone.

Allie handed him the phone, and he studied the image for almost a minute, zooming in and out of the picture.

"Where did you get this?" Lorenzo asked. "I've seen several artifacts and photographs, but never anything quite like this."

Allie looked at Geneva and Ingrid, and both of them nodded.

"We found it in a cave in the mountains," Allie said.

"Was there anything else in the cave? Like wall carvings?" Lorenzo asked.

Ingrid retrieved her phone from her pocket, brought up the photos, and passed it to Lorenzo. He handed Allie back her phone, took Ingrid's, and only looked at it for a few seconds before recognition struck.

"These tusks, this elephant. I've seen images like this before. What you found looks related to Hannibal," said, returning the phone.

"Hannibal who?" Geneva asked.

Lorenzo hesitated before he answered, as if he'd misheard the question. "You've never heard of Hannibal? The Carthaginian general who led the Carthage army against the Roman Republic?"

"Wait, he was the one who took the elephants over the Alps, right?" Ingrid said.

"That's correct," Lorenzo said.

"Can you translate the whole thing or not?" Allie asked.

Lorenzo looked down. On his belt was something that looked like an old-fashioned beeper. He pushed a button to silence the buzzing.

"I'm sorry, I must go. I have other customers to attend to. Tomorrow, I have the day off. If you meet me at the park near the marina at ten in the morning, I will give you exactly what you need." Lorenzo turned to leave.

"And what's that?" Allie asked.

He looked back. "A history lesson. What else?"

## CHAPTER THIRTEEN

At half-past ten, Allie, Geneva, and Ingrid sat together on a bench in the same park where they found the multi-cache the first day they arrived. They'd been on the bench for forty-five minutes, people watching and waiting for Lorenzo.

"I still don't think he's coming," Ingrid said as she impatiently kicked at the ground with the toe of her shoe.

"I don't either. He's late. Let's go," Geneva said.

"Hold on. Why can't you two have a little more patience?" Allie asked.

Geneva turned to Ingrid. "Did your girlfriend just ask the two of us why we can't have a little more patience? Isn't she the one who's always wanting to go so bad she cuts time into half-seconds?"

Ingrid laughed, then nodded. "Yep, that's her. Patience is way outside of her character."

Geneva lowered her voice. "Maybe that's not her."

"Are you thinking pod person? An imperfect duplicate of the Allie we know?"

"Exactly that."

Ingrid and Geneva both leaned forward and looked to their left and found Allie glaring at them.

"Y'all aren't funny," Allie said.

"Ah. No sense of humor," Geneva joked. "Perhaps this is our Allie after all."

Ingrid got the attention of her friends and pointed to a man in the distance. "Is that him? I can't tell."

The women watched as the man with the scarecrow build covered the hundred yards in short order. When he got to within twenty feet, he waved and made a beeline for them.

"Good morning," Lorenzo said. "I apologize for my tardiness. I know the Americans value punctuality. Did you bring the original item with you?"

"We did," Allie said.

"Excellent. Let's move over in that direction. There are tables we can use and spread out more comfortably."

"Lead the way," Allie said.

The women got to their feet and allowed Lorenzo to take the lead. He moved with purpose and had a high energy gait that included a bounce in his step. He didn't wait, and soon outpaced the friends by several steps.

"You go and keep up with him, Allie," Geneva said. "Ingrid and I will get there when we get there."

Allie, who had hung back with the others, increased her speed, and jogged a few feet until she pulled even with Lorenzo.

"We are almost there," Lorenzo said. He raised his hand and pointed. "See, over there in that glade is where we will stop."

Allie looked ahead and saw a half dozen picnic tables. Since the sun was out, and the weather was pleasant, three of the tables already contained occupants. One by a young blond woman reading a book, one with a young mother breastfeeding a baby, and one with two ancient men playing chess.

Lorenzo led Allie to the table farthest away from the others and swung his long legs over the seat and sat. From over his head, he took a weathered brown satchel and placed it on the table.

"Your friends, are they coming?" he asked.

Allie glanced off into the distance and saw Geneva and Ingrid making their way toward her. She watched them for a few seconds. Geneva had brought her cane and relied on it heavily, and Ingrid had a slight limp that was barely perceptible.

"They'll be here shortly. You were too fast for them," Allie said.

"For that, I apologize. I've always been in a rush."

As Lorenzo opened his bag, Allie checked him out. He had thick, long, sandy brown hair that he wore pulled back into a ponytail she hadn't noticed the night before. His eyes were a shade darker than his hair and still had the glint of youth in them. Lorenzo's face had a perfectly straight and slanted nose between his high and prominent cheekbones. His lips were full, yet thin, and when he smiled, he displayed shining white teeth. The only flaw Allie noticed was a slight indention on his front left incisor.

"How are you enjoying Italy?" Lorenzo asked as he cleared out his bag. From it, he extracted two textbooks, a notepad, and two pencils. He checked the tip of one, noticed it had a broken point, and rummaged inside his bag for a sharpener.

"It's a beautiful country," Allie said. "I've never been here before."

"Never been to Italy, and you come to Como? Most first-timers go to Rome or Venice, or Florence. Never to Como."

Allie hesitated for a second before answering. "We were looking for something with fewer tourists, and it's been a long-time dream of mine to visit the Alps."

"And so here you are," Lorenzo said. He finished with the pencil, tapped a finger on the lead to check the point, then, satisfied, set it next to its twin.

"What are you talking about?" Geneva asked as she at last made it to the table and sat down next to Allie. Ingrid took the remaining seat next to Lorenzo.

"Not much. Small talk while waiting for you," Allie said.

"Can I see it?" Lorenzo asked, getting right down to business.

Allie nodded at Ingrid. Ingrid slipped her backpack from her shoulders, undid the zipper, and pulled the parchment from its hiding spot. She handed it to Lorenzo, who took it and gently unrolled it onto the table.

"This is amazing. I've never seen anything like it." He had a giddy quality to his voice, much like a four-year-old on Christmas morning.

"What is it?" Geneva asked.

"Something that should be in a museum if it's authenticated to be real. What it appears to be, based on the writing and the markings on this one side, is an ancient document related to Hannibal," Lorenzo said.

"You mentioned him yesterday," Geneva said. "You have a quick summary you can give us?"

"Sure. Hannibal, like I said, was from Carthage, which is today in Tunisia. He was famous for taking elephants over the Alps to fight the Romans during the Second Punic War."

"Where did he get the elephants from?" Allie asked.

"North Africa. He took them across the Strait of Gibraltar, and attacked Saguntum, in modern day Spain, which touched off the war. Hannibal went through Iberia, then right down Italy's boot. He wreaked havoc in Italy for a decade before he got recalled back to Carthage. He's considered one of the greatest military tacticians in the ancient world."

"Sounds fascinating," Ingrid said.

"It is, actually. And the more I study that period, the more fascinated I am."

"Can you tell us what this says?" Allie asked.

"I can certainly try. Give me a few minutes, and I'll see what I can do."

Lorenzo opened his notebook to a blank page and transferred the writing on the parchment to the notebook. When he finished, he carefully rolled up the item and passed it back to Ingrid. Then he checked the spines of the two books he brought and selected the volume from the bottom of the pile. Without speaking, he worked. To not bother him, the friends remained silent as well, so the only sound came from the turning of pages and scratching of pencil lead across the page.

Several times, Lorenzo seemed to get stuck, and on those occasions, he put the pencil between his teeth as he pulled the book closer and examined the contents. At one point, he pushed the original tome aside and perused the other from cover to almost cover before he found what he sought.

At last, after almost an hour, Lorenzo snapped both books closed and stacked them, then placed his pencils on top of the small pile.

"I've got good news, and bad news, and a bit of a mystery for you," Lorenzo said as he set down his pencil.

"Tell us," Geneva said.

Lorenzo cleared his throat. "Well, the bad news is, although this appears written in Punic and everything appears to point to Hannibal, it isn't from his time."

"How did you determine that?" Geneva asked.

"This isn't all Punic writing on here. There's some neo-Punic, as well as some Latin, and even some Italian thrown in for good measure," Lorenzo said.

"This is all someone's idea of a practical joke?" Ingrid asked.

"Oh, I doubt that. Based on the pictures you showed me of the location where you found this, I doubt anyone would put that much effort into a joke. Besides, this leads to the good news. I would guess this document is from much later, not long ago. In fact, perhaps the early fifteen-hundreds."

"That's not that long ago?" Allie asked.

Lorenzo smiled. "To an Italian, it is practically yesterday.

Italy is the home of the Eternal City, after all."

"So where does the mystery part come from?" Geneva asked.

"From the text. I've translated what I could. My Latin isn't really strong, and I might not have the Italian properly translated since it's a much older dialect than I'm familiar with. Either way, if you want to figure the rest of this message, there's a small local museum in Milan I suggest you visit." Lorenzo referenced his phone and from it jotted down the museum name and address on the page. He tore the entire page from the notebook and handed it to Allie.

Allie looked at the sheet. "Really?"

Lorenzo nodded. "Yes. The text clearly references him by name. Leonardo di ser Piero. Or as we all know him, Leonardo da Vinci."

"I don't understand," Allie said. "Why would an old document written in an ancient language point to Leonardo?"

Lorenzo shrugged, the palms of his hands pointing to the sky. "I don't know. That is your mystery to solve." He looked at his phone and noticed the time. "I'm sorry, but I must go. Good luck with your quest."

Lorenzo gathered his things back into his bag, then shook hands with each of the women before he nodded, turned, and walked away.

Allie looked at the paper, then set it in the center of the table. Ingrid picked it up and read through it before handing it off to Geneva.

"I don't understand any of this," Ingrid said. "What does Leonardo have to do with Hannibal, mountain passes, and heaven valleys?"

"I think you misread that," Geneva said as she looked at the paper. "It says seven valleys, not heaven valleys."

"Okay, then, same question, though," Ingrid said. "None of those things makes sense to me. I mean, they would if they stood separated logically, but if one of my students handed this in as an essay assignment, I'd take one look at it and hand it right back to them."

"Maybe that's the point," Geneva said. "A bit of a riddle to figure out, like a mystery cache. If this thing said to go to this address to locate this thing, that would probably defeat the purpose in the elaborate hiding place in the cave."

Ingrid nodded. "Point taken. So where do we go from here? To Milan? How far is that from here?"

"Only an hour," Allie said. "I'd hate to go down there while Drake is in the hospital. I'd hate for him to get released, only to find out we've skipped town. Why don't we walk back to the hotel and from there we can make a plan of what to do with our day?"

"Can we get lunch? I'm hungry," Geneva said as she rubbed her stomach.

Allie gave two quick nods and was about to speak when her phone rang. She didn't recognize the number but answered anyway. "Hello?"

As she listened, she smiled. "Sure thing. See you soon then." Allie ended the call, then shoved her phone into her pocket. "Lunch will have to wait. That was Drake. They're releasing him."

*

"Are you done with those? Mind if I have them?" Drake asked Allie. He reached forward and grabbed a few French fries from her plate and devoured them without waiting for an answer. "These are fantastic. What do they call them here?"

Allie shrugged as she pushed her plate across the table. "No clue. I asked for French fries, and that's what they gave me. Didn't they feed you in the hospital?"

"They did. Some sort of eggplant thing. Tasted weird to me, but then, I'm not the biggest fan of eggplant. Tell me again what your waiter told you." Drake dipped one fry into a small container of sauce, leaving a drip on the table as he did.

Geneva related the story as she sopped up Drake's mess before he ran his elbow into it. Although he stayed engrossed in his meal, he gave her enough attention to fully take in the story.

"What are we going to do, then?" Drake asked when she finished. Drake wiped his fingers, then pushed the plate aside. "Is there any terrible food in this country? I mean, other than the eggplant?"

"Probably not," Allie said, answering his questions out of order. "Well, we can either continue on our vacation as originally planned, or we can follow this Leonardo thing and see where it goes."

"Couldn't we do both?" Drake asked. "There are geocaches down in Milan, right?"

"Sure, there are," Geneva said. "More than there are around here, actually."

"Any virtual caches?" Ingrid asked.

Geneva shrugged, then retrieved her phone and checked her geocaching app for them. "A dozen or so."

"I vote for both, with an emphasis on virtual caches," Ingrid said.

"Are those virtual caches in the city? No chance of me rolling down a hill or getting mud caked into places where it's impossible to get out without help?" Drake asked.

"I can't tell for sure about the mud part, but they're all within the city. There are a few clustered around the city center, and they radiate out from there."

"What are we waiting for? Let's go," Ingrid said, with a tone that suggested more of an order than a suggestion.

No one argued as they got up from the table and exited the restaurant. Once in the Fiat, Drake climbed into the passenger seat and entered the museum address into Luna and pressed go.

"Are you certain this museum is open?" Drake asked as they pulled away from the curb. "It would be a shame if we drove all the way down there and found out it was closed."

"We called on the way to get you," Allie said. "They're a small museum and usually close by three but will let us in if we're late."

"Can we do this virtual on the way?" Ingrid called from the backseat.

Allie looked in the rear-view mirror and saw Ingrid nodding vigorously at her. Ingrid met her eyes and smiled.

"How complicated is it?" Allie asked.

"There are three sundials on the same block, and we only need to take a selfie with them to get the smiley," Ingrid answered.

"What time is it now?" Allie asked.

"Almost one-thirty."

"Why don't we hit the museum first, then we'll have plenty of daylight left to do all the virtuals you want?"

"Okay, deal," Ingrid said. "You were going to the museum first regardless of what I said, weren't you?" Ingrid added after a few seconds' delay.

Allie grinned, refocused on the road in front of her, and punched the accelerator.

*

"Welcome," the curator said as Allie walked in the door, with Geneva, Ingrid, and finally Drake right behind her.

"Hi. We called earlier today," Allie said.

The curator took her glasses off and placed them on the display case she was sitting behind. She got off her stool, walked around the case, and offered her hand. The woman was short in statue, but her long golden copper hair and infectious smile more than made up for her diminutive size.

"Hello, I'm Victoria. You are Allison?"

"Allie. Yes, we spoke on the phone. We, um, found something that we would like you to take a look at."

Ingrid stepped forward and handed Victoria the parchment.

Victoria eyed the item before she took it, turned around, and unrolled it on the display case.

"This is amazing. I've never seen anything like it," she said. "Where did you find it?"

Ingrid took a few moments to explain geocaching and tell the story of how she found the parchment. Victoria listened intently and nodded her understanding, never removing her gaze from the item.

"I don't know what much of this means. I can only read the Italian parts."

"It's written mostly in Punic," Allie said. She removed the sheet from her pocket, unfolded it, and placed it next to the parchment. "We ran into someone who translated it for us. He says there's also Latin and Italian on there as well."

Victoria nodded. "The Italian pieces are here, and here," she said, pointing to the writing on the parchment. She picked up the paper and studied it. "May I write on this?"

"Sure," Allie answered.

Victoria leaned over a case and grabbed a pencil from a coffee mug featuring a facsimile of Leonardo's *Vitruvian Man*. She leaned over and jotted a few notes, adding in the Italian pieces that Lorenzo had omitted.

"Are you sure that's the correct translation?" Allie asked. "I don't mean to sound rude, but the person who translated the Punic for us said the Italian parts were in an older dialect than he was comfortable with."

Victoria beamed. "Of course it's correct. I've studied Leonardo da Vinci and that time period quite extensively."

"What about the Latin parts?" Geneva asked.

"No, sorry. That I can't help with, but it doesn't look like the missing information obscures the overall message much."

"Can you give us the gist?" Allie asked.

"Certainly. Overall, this document refers to Leonardo di ser Piero da Vinci, or, translated, Leonardo, son of ser Piero from

Vinci. It also mentions something about following the seven valleys to the glorious gift."

"What does that mean?" Drake asked.

Victoria shrugged. "That I can't tell you."

"Does da Vinci have anything to do with this area?" Geneva asked.

Victoria smiled. "Oh, yes. He spent over twenty years in Milan. He painted many important pieces here. In fact, if you go over to the Church of Holy Mary of Grace, you'll find his *Last Supper* in the refectory."

"Really?" Allie asked.

Victoria nodded. "It's only three kilometers from here."

"Does it say anything else about the treasure? Any directions or anything?" Drake asked, jumping to the point.

Victoria studied the writing again. "It says in the next valley, look toward the man in the mountain to guide you."

"You mentioned valleys before," Geneva said. "If there are seven, how would we know which one is the next?"

"Please, wait a moment." Victoria left the room.

While waiting for Victoria to return, Allie took an opportunity to look around at what she could see without leaving the group. Based on a brochure on the counter, the museum featured Leonardo da Vinci's time in Milan, including a historical timeline. It included several photos of the museum's displays on the brochure. Next to the stack of brochures was a map highlighting the different places in Milan where da Vinci roamed, lived, or worked. Allie shoved the brochure and map into her back pocket when she saw Victoria returning.

"I found it," Victoria said. She handed Ingrid the parchment and notepaper, then on the clear countertop, she laid out a topographical map of Italy. "Can you point to where you found this?"

Allie stepped up to the map, found Como, then used her finger to trace the route they'd taken and stopped when she arrived at the mountain trail. "Right about here."

Victoria leaned over and studied the map for a moment. "Okay, yes. In this area, the seven valleys line up almost perfectly from west to east. You were at the far western one, so I suspect it referred to the next closest valley."

"Where would that be?" Drake asked.

Victoria looked again, then put her finger on a location. "The answer you seek would be right here."

# CHAPTER FOURTEEN

Allie rose early the following morning, got dressed, and left the room carrying her shoes, closing the door behind her like a whisper. To the east, the sun had already cleared the two-story building across the street. Despite talking about getting a sunrise start, like the group normally did when out, Allie could tell simply by body language alone that none of her comrades were looking forward to an early morning. By the end of a lengthy discussion, she managed to convince everyone to sleep in for a bit.

While the others slept, Allie took a chair in the lobby and slipped into her favorite hiking boots, laced them up, and headed out the door. She walked to the street, looked to her left and right, and turned to the left. Allie walked down two blocks and took a right, and found the bookstore she remembered passing the day before. When she entered the shop, a little brass bell above her rang.

"May I help you?" the shopkeeper asked.

Allie looked to her left and saw the little man with closely cropped white hair and deep blue eyes. "How did you know I spoke English?"

The shopkeeper tugged at his collar. "I can always recognize a fellow American."

Allie smiled. "Really? Where are you from?"

"Tulsa, Oklahoma originally. I've been in Italy for thirty years. My name is Joseph."

Allie stepped forward and shook his hand. "Nice to meet you. I'm Allie, from Nashville. How did you end up here?"

"Met the love of my life while on a trip to Rome. Got married. Had kids. Opened this little shop. Now, what can I do for you, Allie, from Nashville?"

"I'd like a detailed map, topographic if you have one, specific to northern Italy if you can get that detailed. And a book on Leonardo da Vinci."

Joseph nodded. "The Leonardo section is right behind you. I've got perhaps a dozen titles in English. I'll have to check the map section to check if I have what you want."

Joseph excused himself and headed toward the store's rear, and Allie stepped over to the shelves to check out the Leonardo da Vinci books. When she got there, she found a complete row of them, mostly in Italian, but also in German, English, French, and Chinese. Joseph was correct, and she counted a dozen titles in English. Allie began to page through the options to determine which one gave her a good mix of biographical detail and da Vinci's exploits in Milan. She narrowed it down to two choices and took both books to the counter.

"I have several maps by region. Do you know which regions you're interested in?" Joseph said as he returned to his place, carrying several maps.

"Which region are we in?"

"Lombardy."

"Where does it extend to?" Allie asked.

Joseph opened the map and spread it on his counter. "We are here," he said, pointing at Como. "This region covers about nine-thousand square miles, and most of this part of the country."

"I think this will do nicely. Which one of these two books is the best?" Allie asked, pointing to the tomes on the counter.

Joseph glanced at the titles and picked one up immediately. "This one. It's easier to read, it's a tad more factual, and two euros cheaper."

"I'll take it," Allie said.

Joseph rang her up, and a few minutes later Allie left the shop with her new purchases. She spotted a pastry shop across the street. There, she selected a brioche, a croissant-like pastry filled with custard and a bottle of orange juice and found an empty table. After she had a bite of pastry, she set it to the side and spread open the map before her.

The map was similar to the one that Victoria had, so she quickly found the park location from their previous adventures, as well as the next valley to the east. Allie determined the best road to take there, then retrieved her phone to determine if there were any geocaches in the area. She noticed there was and noted the codes, put her phone away, and closed the map.

Allie took another bite of her brioche and paged through the book on Leonardo da Vinci. The publisher had laid the book out in sections, the first quarter covering the biography of the man, then half the book highlighting the art and inventions he created. The last quarter contained detailed information about his time in Milan. She flipped back to page one and was about to dig in when she heard a muffled ping and felt her table vibrate. Allie extracted the phone and read the text from Ingrid, who was wondering where Allie had slipped off to.

Allie returned the text, stating she'd be back shortly, then scarfed down the rest of her treat and drained the small bottle of juice. Once she'd sufficiently cleaned up the area, Allie headed back to the hotel.

"Where have you been?" Ingrid asked as Allie stepped into

the room.

"Went out for a paper map so we don't get lost again," Allie said.

"Good idea." Ingrid said as she retrieved a brush and started running it through her hair, still wet from the shower she'd just finished.

"Can I take a peek at your leg?" Allie asked.

Ingrid nodded, had a seat on the edge of the bed, and rolled onto her side to give Allie a good view. Allie bent over to inspect Ingrid's leg. The angry redness had lessened to a pinkish color, and there were a couple of quarter-inch lines Allie suspected would be permanent, and one dimple in Ingrid's thigh that looked to be around for the long term.

Allie ran a fingertip gently up Ingrid's thigh, and Ingrid pulled her leg back and laughed in response.

"Stop! That tickles," Ingrid said. She got up from the bed and started to dress.

"Looks like you're fine to me," Allie said.

"I wasn't worried about me," Ingrid said. "I'm more concerned about the other two."

"We'll have to keep a close eye on them today. I think Geneva will be back to normal in a day or two, but Drake is the strong, silent type to a fault and wouldn't complain about his injuries if he had a hole right through his body."

Ingrid nodded as she buttoned her jeans. "I noticed."

Just under two hours later, Allie crested a hill and pulled into a scenic overlook. She stopped the car an inch before she hit the short rock wall before her, and everyone left the Fiat.

"This is an amazing view," Geneva said.

Allie joined Geneva and looked to the horizon. The valley stood lush and green below them, and Allie noticed the road they were currently on wound down the pass and into a small town in the center of the valley. The valley itself appeared to be ten miles long and half as wide.

"You guys want to help us find this cache, or just enjoy the scenery?" Drake asked.

"I guess both," Geneva answered.

Allie turned to her right and caught Drake and Ingrid examining the wall. The rock wall stood three feet high, just high enough to remind drivers to stop the car, and offer an uncomfortable place to sit if someone was so inclined.

"Any hints on this one?" Allie asked.

"No," Ingrid answered. "It has to be somewhere on this wall, though."

Allie glanced around the overlook. It held only four cars, but their Fiat was the only one currently in the lot. There was one sign in Italian, and although she couldn't read it, Allie headed for it anyway and checked behind it, hoping to find a magnetic container of some kind.

"I already checked there," Drake said.

That only left the wall itself. Ingrid, Drake, and Geneva had spread out, looking for gaps or loose rocks within the structure. Allie was about to select a spot to search for herself when Geneva stood up. In her hand, she had a black film container.

"Found it!" Geneva said.

"That wasn't so bad," Drake said.

Geneva passed the log around for signatures and returned it to its hiding spot. When she stood back up, she saw Allie scanning the area.

"What are you looking for?"

"A man in a mountain. Do you see anything?" Allie asked.

Geneva stopped for a moment and looked across the valley. "Nope. Perhaps someone in town can help us out."

Allie slid back behind the wheel and once everyone got strapped in, she navigated down the mountain and into the little town that comprised a gas station with an attached small store and a post office. Out of habit, Allie checked her fuel gauge as she neared the station and pulled into a pump.

"You want me to pump the gas?" Drake asked Allie.

"No. I got it."

"Good. I need to use the restroom. Do you need anything from inside?"

"No."

As Allie filled the tank, the other three headed into the gas station. Geneva was the first one out and she approached Allie with a smile on her face.

"What?" Allie asked.

"I got you a postcard," Geneva said.

The automatic shutoff clicked, so Allie removed the handle, returned it to the pump, and screwed the gas cap back on before accepting the postcard Geneva held out the entire time.

"Thanks," she said as she glanced at it. Allie intended to shove it into her pocket, then took a closer look at it. The picture was black and white and showed an old-time hiker standing in front of a cave entrance. The entrance curled up at either end, making it appear that it was smiling at the photographer. Above the cave were two round boulders that resembled eyeballs.

"The man in the mountain," Allie said in wonder. "Did you ask where this is?"

"Flip the card over."

Allie did and found handwritten directions in Geneva's familiar scrawl.

"Should take us about fifteen minutes from here," Geneva said.

Allie handed the postcard back to Geneva. "You're riding shotgun so you can read these directions as I drive."

Allie and Geneva got into the car and waited impatiently for the others. When Ingrid and Drake finally returned to the car, Allie pulled away a mere second after the final seatbelt clicked into place. Allie followed Geneva's directions, following the main road for almost a mile and then turning right on an unpaved road.

Allie followed the dirt road until it ended at the base of the mountain. The four left the Fiat and walked around a steel barrier that prevented vehicle traffic, and headed up the hill on a narrow dirt path. They arrived at a junction. Geneva checked her directions and led the group to the left. Within a hundred yards, they came to a set of stairs built into the mountain, complete with a wooden handrail broken in several places.

Rather than attempt to use the rotten handrail, they relied on each other to climb the steep stairs. At the top, they found an old sign, too weathered to read. All that remained in print was an outline of a black arrow pointed to the left.

"Well? Shall we?" Geneva asked as she stepped off the path and onto an overgrown trail.

"I'm not so sure we should do this," Ingrid said. "Isn't this the way we got into trouble the other day?"

"It's not raining, so this is a completely different type of trouble," Drake joked.

No one commented on the poor joke. Instead, Geneva focused on the trail before her and kept moving. They progressed up and over a small ridge, then the trail dipped down below a small cliff, and there, staring at them, was the man in the mountain.

"Well, we're here. Now what?" Geneva said.

"That's easy. Now we go in," Drake said.

The group looked at the cave before them. It was just over six feet high in the center and tapered upward on either end and joined with the mountainside. Since no one moved, Drake took the initiative and stepped up to the cave. He stayed just outside and peered in.

"Allie, I don't suppose you brought your flashlight?"

"Of course, I did." Allie, well prepared, took the tiny tool from her pocket, met Drake at the mouth, and turned it on.

Allie shined the light into the cave and saw it was nothing like she anticipated. The previous cave was expansive, with corridors and alternate areas to explore. From the outside, the man on the outside was an interesting sight. The man on the inside, not so much. The interior wasn't so much as a cave than an overhanging shelf, not more than four feet deep on the inside.

"This isn't what I expected," Drake said.

"Me either," Allie admitted. She shone the light from left to right and found nothing but a single offset boulder to the left, one crumpled beer can, and a hastily scribbled heart with the names Marco and Maria in the center. Allie clicked off the light and stowed it in her pocket. She and Drake turned away from the cave and rejoined their friends.

"There's nothing to see," Drake said. "If there ever was in the first place."

"You checked everything? It didn't seem like you were going long enough to check everything," Geneva said.

Allie shook her head. "You can go look for yourself, but there's nothing there."

"Maybe we're missing something," Ingrid said.

"Like what?" Drake asked.

Ingrid shrugged. "I don't know. Maybe we need to read the thing again. What did she say? Look at the mountain man?"

Allie bit her bottom lip and thought for a moment. "No. She said, look toward the man. Toward him. Not at him, or in him. Toward him. Spread out and see if you can find anything that faces this direction."

"I'll bet it's up there," Drake said without moving a muscle. Off to the side was a short, slanted hill that rose forty feet above them. "It's the only possible vantage point from here."

"But there's nothing up there," Geneva said. "It's just trees and brush."

"Sure. It is now, but I'm sure those have grown up sometime over the last five hundred years. I think it's worth a try. Who's with me?"

Drake looked at the women, but no one spoke.

"Actually, No. You're not going up there," Allie said. "I'll go. You shouldn't be scrambling up that hill in your condition."

"But," Drake started.

Geneva held up a single finger in front of his face. "Allie's right. You're grounded, mister. I'll go with her."

"Me too," Ingrid said.

Drake huffed, but everyone ignored him as Allie took point and walked fifty feet to the bottom of the rise. She stopped and looked up at the hill, which appeared a little steeper than it did from the original vantage point.

"Okay, let's do this," she said to the women as she found a spot between two large rocks and started the climb.

Allie followed her usual method of climbing hills, picking out a path visually before moving an inch. Slowly, she made her way up the slope, avoiding rocks, boulders, and trees as she ascended. She stopped after a few yards and looked behind her. Allie spotted Geneva following her exact path, and Ingrid was only a few steps behind Geneva. She turned back around and plowed forward, stopping only once when she deemed the path she'd chosen to be too hard on Geneva and Ingrid.

Allie made a final push, and the ground evened out on an outcropping eight feet wide by ten feet long. She turned around once she got settled on her feet and offered a hand to Geneva and finally Ingrid.

"Splendid view," Geneva said.

Allie stood and looked out across the area. Through the trees, she picked out half of the mountain man, and saw Drake standing on the trail waiting for them. He paced back and forth, which Allie knew from experience was from impatience.

"Can I have your flashlight?" Ingrid asked Allie. Without thinking, Allie handed it to her, and Ingrid switched it on and stepped away.

Allie turned and saw Ingrid headed for the back wall of the outcropping. There, she saw not so much of a cave as an unnaturally round hole in the stone, the approximate size of a sewer hole cover.

Ingrid got to her knees and shined the light into the hole.

"There's a little opening in here," she said.

Without a second of hesitation, Ingrid crawled into the hole.

"There's no way I would have done that," Geneva said to Allie.

Allie shook her head. "That girl does some odd things sometimes."

From outside, Allie and Geneva watched as Ingrid moved her legs and pushed farther in. Only the soles of Ingrid's shoes remained in sight. After a few minutes, Ingrid's feet wiggled, and Allie heard a muffled noise from inside. She stepped closer to the hole.

"What?" Allie called in. Allie got the message and nodded. "She wants us to pull her out."

Allie took Ingrid's right leg, and Geneva stepped up and took the left, and on the count of three, Allie and Geneva slowly pulled their friend from the breach.

"Thanks for the hand," Ingrid said as she stood. The front of her clothes were a mix of tan and gray from the dust, and when she patted herself down, she produced a cloud that Allie and Geneva had to step back from.

"How was that?" Geneva asked. "Did you find anything in there?"

"Not much. There were mostly rocks, a couple of old spider webs, and a really interesting skeleton of some small animal. Might have been a raccoon or squirrel or something, but all that's left is bone."

"That's it? Bones and rocks?" Geneva said. "I guess we struck out again."

"Oh, wait, there was this in there, too," Ingrid said. She bent over, reached into the hole, and from it extracted a bronze box that glinted in the sunlight.

# CHAPTER FIFTEEN

Ingrid shoved the box into her backpack, and the women picked up Drake on the hike back to the car. Once there, Ingrid retrieved the box and set it on the hood of the Fiat.

"This is amazing, isn't it?" Ingrid said. A layer of tarnish in warm brown tones covered the box, but that didn't affect the beauty. There were intricate designs of common animals on every side. One side featured a horse, one a chicken, one a dog, and the fourth a cow. The top had an etching of all four animals together.

"Open it," Drake said.

Ingrid picked up the shoebox-sized box and attempted to lift the lid. It didn't budge. She made a second attempt, failed, and handed the box to Drake.

"You do it," Ingrid said.

Drake tried to lift the lid, but couldn't. He brought the box to eye height and scrutinized it.

"I don't see any seams or hinges at all. Are you sure this is a box?" he said.

Ingrid took it back and tipped it from side to side. Everyone heard the sound of something shifting from within.

"There's something in it," Ingrid said. "It must be a box of some kind. We just need to figure out how we open it."

"Might I suggest a hammer?" Drake asked.

Ingrid pulled the box back. "No way. You're not taking a hammer to this relic. It's probably priceless. What should we do?"

"Let's go back to the museum," Geneva suggested.

At four-thirty, Allie parked the car in the tiny lot attached to the museum. Ingrid had called along the way, so Victoria stood waiting by the door to let them in. She led the group into the small room that functioned as half break room and half storage room. There was a long table in the room, half-covered with papers. Victoria cleaned up the area and scavenged enough chairs for everyone to sit. Once everyone had a seat, Victoria removed her glasses and set them down before her.

"You said on the phone you had something exciting to show me?" Victoria said, leaning over the table.

Ingrid retrieved the box and set in on the table in front of Victoria.

Victoria's hands covered her mouth. "Oh, my. Do you know what this is?"

"A box," Ingrid answered. "We don't know how to open it, though."

Victoria laughed. "A box. No, dear. This is more than just a simple box."

Without excusing herself, Victoria pushed away from the table and stood up with such force that the chair she sat in toppled backward and hit the floor with a clatter. She left the room in a hurry while the four remained at the table, seated and silent. After a matter of several minutes, Victoria returned carrying a large book that she set down at her place. She picked up her chair and settled back into it.

"What do you have there?" Drake asked.

"In this volume are sketches of objects and inventions attributed to Leonardo da Vinci. I say attributed because none were ever confirmed. In here is a box similar to yours."

Victoria turned the book around so everyone could see it. The sketch on the page showed a three-dimensional box, and around the edges were clouds with faces, puffed cheeks blowing wind outward.

"These are clouds," Geneva said, pointing to the book. "Ours has animals."

"Yes. This one represents the direction of the four winds. But rumor has it there were different etchings. Like these clouds, or your animals, or stars in the sky. The method for entry was all the same. All you needed was a…." Victoria looked around the table and didn't find what she looked for. She lifted the book to check underneath, then replaced the book and left the room again. She returned a few minutes later, carrying something between her fingers that looked like a thin knitting needle.

"In theory, this should work the same as the one in the book."

Victoria put on her glasses and turned the box on its side so the chicken was facing up. She lined up the needle with the chicken's eye, then pushed down. There was a barely audible click, and Victoria grinned. She turned the box, so the next animal was facing up, then shoved the needle into the eye. Once she'd finished every animal, she flipped the box, so the bottom was up. She pulled on the bottom, and it released. Remaining on the table was the box top and four slats with tiny pegs that lined up perfectly with the animal eyes.

"Do you want to do the honors? It's your box," Victoria said.

Ingrid stepped forward and picked the small piece of parchment from the box and gently unrolled it on the table. For comparison, Allie found the sheet from the previous parchment and laid that to the side.

"It looks the same as the other one to me," Allie said after studying the two documents.

Victoria leaned over the table to get a better view. "Similar, yes, but different in places. And this one is all in Italian. No Punic, no Latin."

"Can you translate it for us?" Allie asked.

"I can. Give me a few minutes," Victoria said. She took the parchment and stood. "Do you mind if I take this with me to my desk?"

"Not at all. Do you mind if I come with you?" Allie said. "I won't get in the way."

Victoria nodded. "Of course, follow me."

Allie followed Victoria from the room, through the museum, and to a small office close to the front door. Victoria took a seat behind an oak desk, cluttered with papers, books, a half-empty coffee cup, and a laptop.

Allie looked around for a chair, didn't spot one, and instead found a seat on a gray metal two-drawer file cabinet. From her position, it was easy to look over Victoria's shoulder to see what she was up to.

The first thing Victoria did was copy the text from the parchment to a legal pad, skipping two lines as she did so. When she had the lines copied, she rolled up the parchment and handed it over to her shoulder to Allie, who took it and placed it in her lap. Then, she went to work on the translation.

"Hand me that book you're almost sitting on, will you?" Victoria said.

Allie moved forward, reached behind her, and found the book wedged back behind her. She glanced briefly at the title, but as it was in Italian, she didn't know what it said. Allie handed it to Victoria.

Victoria opened the book and shuffled through a few pages until she found the page she wanted. With her index finger as a guide, she traced it down the page until she arrived at the word she needed. She copied the word to the page, closed the book, and pushed it aside. For twenty minutes, Victoria worked on the translation while Allie shifted on top of the cabinet, trying to get comfortable. At last, Victoria dropped her pencil and turned her seat to face Allie.

"I'm finished. This is quite fascinating. Should we rejoin your friends?"

Victoria didn't wait for an answer. Instead, she rose and exited the room. Allie followed close on her tail, and although Victoria made only a slight detour within the museum to track down a book, she rushed right back to the conference room.

"We thought you guys left," Drake said as Allie and Victoria entered the room.

"Sorry, that took me longer than I expected," Victoria said as she took her chair. "This dialect is five hundred years old, so it takes a little while to get it correct."

Allie stretched, then dropped into her chair. She passed the parchment to Ingrid, who set it back in the box, then aligned the lid, and closed it.

"How familiar are you with the lost treasures of Leonardo?" Victoria asked.

Victoria looked around the table. No one reacted to the question.

"Tell us," Geneva said.

Victoria held up the book she'd retrieved. "This book is called *Mysteries of the Masters*. In essence, it is a compilation of random theories, secrets, and legends of the classical Italian painters. Caravaggio, Michelangelo, Raphael, Donatello, Leonardo."

"So, all the turtles?" Drake asked.

Victoria cocked her head and looked at him. "Turtles?"

"Forgive his poor joke," Geneva said. "Please go on. He won't interrupt again."

"Among the author's claims is that Leonardo, during his last years in Milan, hid away much of his art, journals, and inventions, and to this day, no one has ever found them."

Allie raised an eyebrow. "How can that be? Wasn't Leonardo one of the most prolific renaissance men of the times? Didn't he produce like hundreds of things over his lifetime?"

"Yes, but although the public knows about many of them, there's really no way to tell what he created over the course of his lifetime."

"But why hide things?" Ingrid asked.

Victoria shrugged. "I don't know. The answer to that question is long lost to history. And there's always the more certain answer, that there is nothing hidden, and they already found everything there is to find."

"That doesn't explain this, though," Ingrid said, placing her hand on top of the box. "Why go through all the trouble of hiding these clues if they didn't lead somewhere?"

"It could be a hoax," Drake said. "I mean, it's not like we've had any of these things authenticated. Someone could have made those parchments last month and found a way to make them look aged. And anyone with a basic working knowledge of metals could have cobbled that box together."

"But what about the cave where I found the first parchment?" Ingrid asked. "That seemed too elaborate and involved to be a simple prank. That would be like building an entire house to hide a geocache in a brick within the foundation."

Drake considered the point for a moment. "Okay, I think you have me there."

"There is a way to get your answer," Victoria said. "I have a colleague who can test those items for you, and you'll know if they're authentic or not."

"When?" Allie asked.

"Please wait here while I make a phone call," Victoria said. She excused herself from the room.

Allie leaned over and picked up the legal pad.

"What does it say? Is there any clue to find the next stop?"

Geneva asked.

"Past two, the master's mind awaits beneath the witch's cap," Allie read.

"That's it? You guys were gone for a half hour for a single line?" Drake asked.

"No. There's other stuff in here about glory and riches and having to be worthy to walk in the footsteps of the greatest man ever. But I skipped all that stuff. There's only one line about where to go next."

"What does 'past two' mean?" Ingrid asked. "Past two what?"

"Valleys, I imagine," Victoria said while she entered the room, catching the last part of the conversation. "My friend can meet with you soon if you're willing to stay longer."

"We'll stay," Drake said. "Why skip two valleys?"

"I mentioned there are seven valleys, correct? The first where you found the parchment, and the second where you found this box? That suggests you are supposed to be headed west to east, and the next two valleys in the line are unsettled by man."

"Why is that?" Allie asked.

"The third valley is nothing but a lake during the summer months, fed by snowmelt from the north."

"The entire valley?" Drake asked.

"Yes. It's not a large one, perhaps two or three kilometers square."

"And it's always been that way? Someone building a dam somewhere did not create the lake?" Allie asked.

"No. It's been like that for as long as people have been in this region," Victoria said.

"What about the fourth valley?" Drake asked.

"That valley is impassible. It's more of a bowl than a valley. The mountains on every side are almost vertical. You can't get in there without climbing gear, and climbers are the only people who generally visit there.

"So, we can't drive there?" Geneva asked.

Victoria shook her head. "No. You can't access that valley without ropes, a parachute, or a helicopter."

"And thus, we skip two and go to the fifth valley?" Allie asked.

Victoria nodded. "Yes. It's a valley much like the one you've just returned from. There's a medium-sized village there. It has a restaurant, several houses within town, a store, and a church. It's quite a lovely town. It's not a large valley, smaller than where you were today." Victoria glanced at a clock on the wall above the coffeemaker. "We should go if you want to meet with my friend. Her place is only a few blocks from here, so we can walk."

The group rose as one and while the friends moved toward the front door, Victoria circled around the museum and turned out the lights. Once they were all outside, Victoria pointed in the direction they needed to go.

Allie walked ahead with Victoria while Drake, Geneva, and Ingrid trailed behind.

"There are a lot of Leonardo da Vinci sites in Milan?" Allie asked, more like a statement than a question.

"Oh, yes. There are many places here you can go to see his work. There's a fresco of his at the castle, although that's been under restoration for many years and not often open for viewing. You can see his *Codex Atlanticus* at the Biblioteca Ambrosiana. It's quite fascinating, although they only display a few pages at a time. And if you go to the National Museum of Science and Technology, you can see several models based on his designs."

"That doesn't sound like a lot," Allie said.

"Sadly, Leonardo's work is spread all over the world, so no one has access to the entire breadth of it. But what we do have access to here in Italy is remarkable."

Allie nodded in agreement and stopped speaking. As they crossed the street, she spotted a square. It was a patch of green surrounded by the bustle of the city, lined with waist-high bushes. A sidewalk divided the grass and led to a statue of someone Allie didn't recognize. Bordering the grass were four park benches, spread out equally to maintain an esthetic balance, and on one bench sat a man engrossed in a book. Somehow, on the busy road filled with speeding cars and beeping mopeds, the man found a quiet spot to read. Allie thought of her book back at the hotel.

Allie paid so much attention to the reading man she didn't notice Victoria had turned a corner and almost walked right onto the street into the path of an oncoming bus. She felt a sudden jerk on her jacket collar, one that pulled her back, startled.

"Where are you going?" Drake asked, releasing the grip on her coat.

The bus sped up, leaving a puff of exhaust behind.

"Thanks. I was daydreaming, I guess," Allie said.

"Come on. We're falling behind."

Allie looked around the corner and saw Victoria was almost a half block ahead of them, unaware the rest of the group had stopped. As if by telepathy, she halted, turned around, and waited. Once the group caught up, Victoria pointed to a nondescript door.

"We're here," Victoria said. She reached for the bell.

The bell shrilled, and the group waited for almost a full minute before the door opened. A tall woman with brown hair flowing down to her waist stepped outside and swept Victoria in her arms. The friends greeted each other with kisses on each cheek.

"These are your people?" the woman asked. "Please come inside."

"I'm Lucia," the woman said, greeting Allie with kisses as well.

"I'm Allie. That's Geneva, Drake, and Ingrid," Allie said, introducing her friends who had instinctively lined up to enter the building.

Allie followed Victoria, fully expecting to be led into the interior of a house, but instead the main room looked more like a chemistry lab than a house. There was a giant dining table in the middle, and Lucia had the walls lined with file cabinets, storage cabinets, and workstations topped with clusters of beakers, microscopes, and several things that looked like microwave ovens.

"So, what do you have for me?" Lucia said when she'd ushered Ingrid into the room.

"We have some things we found, and we'd like to know if you can authenticate them," Allie said.

Lucia laughed in a pitch that resembled a meadowlark song. "I can. It is what I do, among my other tasks."

Allie nodded at Ingrid, who slipped her backpack from her shoulders, undid the straps, and pulled out the parchment and the box.

"Where did you get these?" Lucia asked.

"The parchment we found accidentally while out hiking. The box we found based on what was on the parchment," Allie said.

Lucia stared at Allie for a moment, and when Allie didn't provide further information, Lucia grinned. "Let's see what we can find out."

Lucia stepped to the corner near the door, where she put an oversized lab coat over the dark blue dress she wore and donned a pair of thin gloves. She pulled out a stool from under the table, sat down, and carefully unrolled the parchment.

"Oh, this is lovely," Lucia said. "You have quite the find here."

Lucia stretched to her left and retrieved a container stuffed with long cotton swabs and an unmarked white plastic bottle filled with a liquid.

"This won't damage your piece, okay?" Lucia said to no one

in particular. She selected a swab, put two drops of liquid on the swab's cotton tip. She rubbed the tip on the parchment, blackening the cotton.

Satisfied, Lucia moved to one of her workstations, where she prepared her sample and dropped it into a machine.

"What is that?" Drake asked.

"It is a mass spectrometer. It will help determine what they made this ink from."

"How long will that take?" Drake asked.

Lucia smiled again. "It works quickly, and I should have the results in only a day or two. In the meantime, let's check the parchment itself."

With a pair of scissors and permission, Lucia snipped a tiny sample from the document and placed it beneath a microscope. "Ah, yes. They made this from ibex hide."

Lucia returned to the table and turned her attention to the box.

"You'll need something thin, like a needle, to open that," Victoria said.

Lucia rose and checked around the lab until she found something to use, then handed it to Victoria, who opened the box. Once inside, Lucia repeated the tests with the second parchment. Once she finished, she examined the box itself.

"Do you need to run that through the machine, too?" Geneva asked.

"No. There are more practical tests I can do," Lucia said.

Lucia circled the room again and returned with several items to the table.

"This is a magnet," she said, holding up the object for all to see. She placed it against the box, and it didn't stick. "That is a good sign. Bronze is non-magnetic."

Next, she took a small silver hammer, held the box lid loosely by a corner, and tapped the lid. A tone, not unlike a bell, resounded in the room for a few seconds.

"Pleasant, yes?" Lucia said. "I'm quite certain this is bronze."

For her last test, Lucia took several minutes to examine the box with a magnifying glass, while the rest of the group stayed silent and waited.

"This is remarkable construction. It is definitely hand etched," Lucia said.

She went into another bout of silence for several minutes, then she looked up, her eyes wild with excitement.

"Oh, my goodness!" Lucia exclaimed. "Yes!" She jumped from the stool and circled the table, unable to control her emotions.

"What is it?" Victoria asked.

Lucia returned to the box and held the magnifying glass for her. "What do you see?"

Victoria moved the glass to focus it better, then sat straight up. "Look at this," she said to Allie.

Allie came forward, looked through the glass and saw what looked like four little loops connected to each other. "Yeah? So?"

Victoria grinned. "Leonardo never signed his artwork. Instead, he used a symbol of intertwining knots. I believe this to be genuine."

<h1 style="text-align:center">CHAPTER SIXTEEN</h1>

The group headed out before sunrise the next morning.

"I hope this isn't a sign of things to come," Ingrid said as she looked out the window at the falling rain. "Usually I like the rain, but for this trip, I'm pretty much over it."

"I second that," Drake said. "Rain, rain, go away, and don't come back until I'm back home in my living room."

"Oh, come one. It's barely a sprinkle. Just a passing cloud, really," Allie said. "If it makes you feel any better, it should stop raining in an hour or so. The weather segment on the news this morning said it will be warmer and sunny today."

"How far is it to the valley?" Drake asked.

"If we take the straight shot, it will be just under three hours. If we stop for the caches that Geneva researched for us, we could easily add another hour to that time. The question becomes, should we do the caches along the way, or just head straight for the valley?"

"How hard are the caches?" Drake asked.

"You'd have to ask Geneva that question," Allie said.

"Geneva? How hard are they?" Drake asked from the

passenger seat. When he received no answer, he repeated her name. "Ingrid, is everything okay back there?"

Ingrid glanced over at her seatmate. Geneva reclined back in her seat, her head pressed against the window, and had her jacket covering her like an impromptu jacket. As they drove under a streetlight, Ingrid noticed Geneva's chest rise and fall.

"She's napping, Drake. Did you keep her up too late?" Ingrid asked.

"I don't know. She stayed up reading while I drifted off to sleep. Actually, a nap sounds nice," Drake said.

"You can't nap, you're the navigator," Allie whispered in a low tone. "You know the rules."

"Ingrid can do it," Drake said.

"I can do it," Ingrid offered.

Allie didn't answer, and instead pulled into the parking lot of a closed business. Once stopped, Ingrid and Drake switched seats. Allie listened for Ingrid's seatbelt to click and then watched in the rearview as Drake got settled. Like Geneva, he rested his head against the window and closed his eyes.

"Those guys are no fun," Allie said as she pulled back onto the road.

"I think they're both still messed up from a few days ago. Drake was barely keeping up with us yesterday. Did you notice?"

"I did. Is there something going on that he's hiding from us? Surgery complications, perhaps? Has Geneva said anything about him?"

"No," Ingrid said. "Well, yes. She mentioned he's been sleeping more, but she blew that off to jet lag and all the running around we've been doing."

"Funny, I think we've been running around less here than we would be back home. Has he been taking his antibiotics?" Allie asked.

"I don't know. We'll have to remember to ask him. Do you think he'll tell us the truth about it?"

"Good question. He's as honest as anyone can be, but occasionally he gets that macho-induced dose of irrationality,"

"Maybe we should steal his pills and count them. That would tell us right away if he's taking them or not," Ingrid said.

"Although that's a great idea, it's dishonest. We'll ask him and trust that he'll tell us the truth."

"What if we had Geneva steal and count? They're in the same room. He wouldn't even notice."

Allie smiled. "That's an even better idea. You want to ask her, or should I?"

"I will, first chance I get. So, back to the initial question. Do we stop for the geocaches along the way, or head directly to the valley?"

"She has the list, so let's see how far we get before she wakes up. Personally, I'd like to find one on the way, if only to get out of the car and stretch the legs."

Allie approached the highway she needed, flipped on her signal, turned right, and began the slow climb into the mountains. Through the raindrops and the intermittent windshield wipers, Allie noticed the first sign of the approaching sun, a swatch of brightening colors attempting to climb the mountains before her.

"I love sunrises," Allie blurted.

"Me too," Ingrid said. "Especially over the mountains, or a large body of water."

Allie retreated into her own thoughts and split her concentration between the road and the sunrise. As the miles dropped behind her, the sun advanced in the sky. The rays stretched over the mountaintops, and the rain ended for good as shades of pink, orange, and gold chased away the drops and replaced them with the promise of a bright day. During her trance, the miles and night sky drifted away as lazy as a napping cat.

"The rain stopped," Drake said.

Allie glanced into the mirror and caught him rubbing his nap from his eyes. "I told you it would."

"There's a geocache at a gas station two miles up the road. Can we stop there?" Geneva asked.

"No problem," Allie said, straightening her posture. "It's a perfect time for a break."

As she entered into the station, Allie determined she had plenty of gas, so she pulled into a parking space rather than a pump.

"I have to go use the restroom," Ingrid said as she exited the car.

Drake accompanied Ingrid into the building while Allie followed Geneva. Geneva's GPS guided them around the side of the building, and there, Geneva spotted the geocache right away. The geocache stood out in plain sight, a flat magnet a little larger than a bumper sticker attached to the side of the air compressor. The magnet looked official and although it contained words in Italian neither woman recognized, it also held the identification number of the geocache.

Geneva removed the magnet and flipped it over. There she found the long flat log tucked inside a plastic bag taped to the magnet. She fished it out, signed it, and handed it to Allie.

"How's Drake doing?" Allie asked as she penned her nickname on the log.

Geneva's eyes met Allie's. "He seems a little off. I've asked him about it several times, but he just waves me away and tells me he's fine."

Allie nodded. "Has he been taking his meds?"

Geneva hesitated before answering. "I'm not sure. I think he took his pills yesterday. He's supposed to take the antibiotics twice a day with meals."

"We've spent all our meals together, and I've yet to see him take a pill," Allie said.

"I usually take them after," Drake said.

Allie and Geneva turned around, not realizing Drake and Ingrid had joined them.

Drake got the bottle out of his pocket and shook it. Inside, the pills rattled. "Trust me, the last thing I want is an infection."

"We're just concerned. Have you been doing okay?" Allie asked.

"Sure. Other than being a little more tired than usual, but my doctor said I should expect that."

Allie stood, unresponsive. "Okay, if you say so," she said at last, passing the log and pen to Drake. Allie shivered, regretting she'd left her jacket in the car rather than putting it on. Geneva and Ingrid were wearing theirs to ward off the early morning chill.

"I'm heading back to the car," Allie said. "I need to put on my coat, so I'll meet y'all back there." As she looked up, Allie noticed a bead of sweat on Drake's forehead.

Over an hour later, the road wound its way around a bend, and before them, the valley they'd searched for came into view. Even though they were a few miles from town, they could easily spot the church steeple towering over the rest of the town. They passed a sign announcing the village limits when Ingrid's phone rang.

"Hello? I'm sorry I don't speak… Yes? Okay. Yes, I understand. Thank you." Ingrid disconnected the call. "That was Lucia. She said her analysis is done, and the ink is consistent with what they made during Leonardo's lifetime. She says that although she can't a hundred percent validate the results without further tests, she's about eighty percent confident in her assessment."

"I'll take eighty," Allie said. "Anyone have an idea of how to find the witch's cap?"

"I do. Enter these coordinates into Luna," Geneva said. She relayed the numbers and Ingrid entered them into the machine and pressed go.

"What is this?" Allie asked.

"There's a geocache there. In the description, it mentions that the cache is located along a popular hiking trail that leads to one of the unique geological features in the area. It turns out that there's a geological feature there that looks like an isosceles triangle. To me, if you put an isosceles triangle on top of a wide brim, what does that look like?"

Ingrid grinned. "A witch's hat."

Geneva nodded. "Exactly. That's what I thought of as well."

"I'm just worried that if there's a geocache there and it is a popular hiking spot, that someone would have discovered the cave a long time ago," Allie said.

"The cache itself is an EarthCache, so there's no physical container to find," Geneva said.

"How hard are the questions?" Drake asked.

"Not bad, actually. We should be able to figure it out once we get there."

Allie continued the drive, and once she got to the far side of town, the road followed a small river. Luna advised Allie to turn right, and when she did, Allie drove over a stone bridge, turned left, and continued following the river from the opposite side of the main road. Eventually, the river curled away from the main road, and Allie followed the path they were on until they reached a marked parking area. Allie pulled in and shut down the Fiat.

"Okay, Geneva, where do we go from here?" Allie asked once they were all outside and ready to go.

Geneva checked her GPS and pointed at the only trail leading from the parking lot and toward the mountainside. "I think we go that way. It's not far, only four hundred feet or so."

"It's always the 'or so' part that makes me nervous," Drake said.

Geneva grabbed Drake's arm and dragged him forward. "Let's go, hero. I'm sure this won't be any trouble at all."

Ingrid laughed. "Always the famous last words, right?"

Geneva walked to the trailhead and stepped into the trees. Unlike the previous trails they'd been on recently, this one had a layer of asphalt paving the way. In several spots, wooden horse fences kept the hikers from venturing off the trail. At one point the trail veered off toward the river, and the slope changed, forcing the friends to trudge uphill for a hundred feet. Once the climb ended, the trees cleared away, and they came to an open area.

"Wow, that's cool," Drake said, looking at the geological features before them.

Carved by nature into the mountain was a shape that looked like a perfect triangle. It stood forty feet high and, on either side, water flowed from the mountain above. Before them, the trail continued on beneath the triangle. One side of the path butted up against the mountain, and on the opposite side, a black steel fence prevented anyone from falling over the edge.

"Should we do the EarthCache first, or look for a cave?" Drake asked.

"Let's get the questions out of the way. They'll only take a couple of minutes," Geneva suggested. "The questions are: what are the angle of the two long sides of the triangle, what color are the vertical veins of stone beneath the triangle with the number of each, and what happens to the water that falls on either side of the hat?"

"I'll take the angle question," Ingrid said.

"I'll do the vein count," Allie offered.

"So then, I guess I'll check out the water," Drake said.

Ingrid took her phone from her pocket and found the protractor app she wanted. She held her phone up before her with the phone lined up with the triangle's side, then walked beneath the triangle and took the measurement from the other side. She returned to Geneva.

"I've got seventy-five degrees on both sides, give or take," Ingrid said.

Geneva nodded and typed the information into her phone. "Got it."

As Ingrid stepped away to help Allie, Drake returned.

"The water on both sides falls from here and joins into the main river," Drake said.

Geneva recorded his answer, then they moved to the thirty-foot-wide area beneath the triangle.

"Do you have an answer, Allie?" Geneva asked.

Allie stood at the opposite end from Geneva. "I'm doing a third count. I came up with difference numbers on the first two."

Allie looked at the wall behind her, and she scanned the vertical stripes in alternating black and red-brown in the shaded area beneath the triangle. The stripes had different widths, and Allie touched each stripe as she counted them aloud and walked in Geneva's direction.

"I've got forty black and thirty-eight in whatever you would call this reddish-brown," Allie said.

"Okay, got it."

"What do you suppose those stripes are?" Ingrid asked.

"I don't know," Allie said. "Probably exposed mineral veins or something. Take a picture of them and we'll figure it out later."

"You know what I didn't see in here anywhere? A cave," Drake said.

"I didn't either," Allie said.

"That last one I found wasn't in a cave. It was just a hole, remember?" Ingrid said. "Everyone spread out and see if you can find anything at all."

Ingrid, Drake, and Geneva started to examine the wall behind them while Allie stepped to the fence, leaned over, and looked below. She saw a drop of fifteen feet, and then the river as it meandered its way toward the village. She leaned over farther and looked to the left and right to see if there was a way down to the ground and spotted the remnants of an old trail.

Allie followed the main trail to the opposite side of the

triangle. There, the trail ended, enclosed by more steel fencing. She went to the river's side of the fence and looked down the mountain. There, she spotted a set of long disused stone steps carved into the granite. The steps were rugged, covered with gray-green lichen, and looked perilous from where she stood. Allie looked back at her friends who were still examining the back wall, then shrugged, and slipped easily through the fence rails.

The first stair down was wide and dry, and Allie had no difficulty stepping down. The next step, although dry, was barely the width of one sideways foot, so Allie held on to the bottom fence rail to help her down. From there, Allie carefully climbed down another two stairs before she decided it seemed safer to sit and go down one step at a time. Feet, then butt. She repeated the process a dozen times, and then the steps made a turn toward the river. She looked ahead and, to her delight, saw the steps led to an outcropping wide enough to support not only her, but all of her friends if they chose to join her.

Allie turned and faced the vertical wall behind her, looking for any caves, holes, or indents in the wall. She found nothing, so she stepped backward three feet, making sure she was well enough from the edge, and scanned the area with her eyes, looking for any visual clues. She was about to give up and head back to her friends when she spotted something where the third step intersected with the wall, something that resembled a patterned scar.

Allie crouched and ran her finger over the postage-stamp shaped spot. Something about it seemed familiar, so she found a flat stone and used it to scrape away the collected dirt and algae. When the surface seemed somewhat clean, she dropped to her knees and looked at it closer.

"I found something, I think," Allie called out.

"Allie? Where are you?" Ingrid yelled back.

"I'm down below. Look over the edge."

Allie stood and looked up, and after a couple of seconds, Ingrid's face beamed down at her.

"What are you doing down there?" Ingrid asked.

"I found something," Allie yelled, pointing at the mark. "Come down here. No wait. Stay there."

Allie retrieved a phone, snapped a picture, then sent it to Ingrid via a text, added a brief message and waited for the response. She looked above her and saw Ingrid's head disappear. After a few moments, Ingrid returned.

"Yes, that looks like the knots. Geneva and Drake think so too. Should one of us come down?" Ingrid yelled.

"No. Give me a minute," Allie yelled.

Allie found the car keys and used them to scrape away the caked-in dirt from the knots, and as she did, the small indent grew deeper. She dropped to her knees, leaned forward and blew on the symbol. Eventually, enough of the dirt cleared out and the details within the pattern became obvious. A hole was in the center of the intertwined knots. Allie used her little finger to clear the dirt from the hole, then looked around and found a stick that looked small enough to fit in the void. Allie continued working on the dirt, then put the stick in the hole to determine how deep it went. She felt some resistance, pushed harder, and heard something click. When she tried to remove the stick, it stuck. She pulled harder, and to her surprise, the entire section of wall around the symbol broke away.

Allie turned, switched on her phone light and shone it in the hole. Inside, she spotted a leather bag. She removed it, opened the bag, and withdrew a parchment. Allie unrolled it and saw it was similar to the two others in their possession, so she returned it to the bag and returned to her feet.

She looked up and saw everyone watching her with interest.

"I'm coming back up," Allie yelled to the group. She felt their gaze on her as she carefully ascended each step. When she got to the top, she handed Geneva the bag, and Drake helped her back through the fence.

"Another parchment?" Ingrid asked.

"Yes. Of course, it looks like it's all in Italian again," Allie said.

"We should have brought Victoria along. That way, we could have saved time running all the way back to Milan," Drake said.

"There's no reason to run. We'll send her a picture of the parchment, and she can work from that. We can stay out here and head over to the next valley," Geneva said.

"Let's head back to the village. We'll get something to eat while we wait for Victoria's answer," Ingrid said.

Allie nodded. "I hope it's somewhere that sells gelato. "

CHAPTER SEVENTEEN

"I'm sorry they didn't have any gelato," Ingrid said to Allie. "Are you sure you don't want a bite of this cannoli? It's quite delicious."

Allie shook her head while she bit into the last of her sandwich. She swallowed and washed it down with a drink of orange soda that tasted more like an orange than anything she'd ever experienced in America.

"Did you get the translation back yet?" Allie asked as she capped her bottle.

Ingrid put down her dessert and picked up her phone. "Nope. She said it would be a bit. Perhaps a bit hasn't elapsed yet."

Allie wiped her hands with a napkin and dropped it onto her plate. "All this waiting is maddening for me. I feel like I should be doing something."

"You can do something. Be patient. I'm trying to finish my lunch," Ingrid said. "Perhaps you should go out for a walk like the other two did."

Allie looked out the restaurant window but didn't spot her

friends. The only people in view were an old man walking a dog and the woman he was talking to. "Where did you say they headed?"

"I didn't say, and neither did they. Geneva said they would be back within a half hour."

"How long have they been gone?" Allie asked.

Ingrid consulted her phone. "Twenty-one minutes. Chill out. You're driving me nuts." Ingrid placed her phone to her right and returned to her cannoli. "You sure you don't want the last bite? You don't know what you're missing."

"I do. I'm missing gelato," Allie said. "Chocolate. Strawberry. Mint. Peach. Whatever. Gelato is what I'm missing the most."

Ingrid smiled. "We'll get you some. I promise." She slowly ate the last of her dessert and followed it with the last of a glass of milk. "Hey, I have an idea. Why don't we head over to the next valley? We know the clue is going to lead there anyway, so why not get a jump on it? We might see if there are any geocaches over there and collect those while we wait on Victoria."

Allie nodded. "That's a good idea. And you've got milk on your chin."

While Ingrid wiped her mouth, Allie opened her backpack and fished out the map. It took her a moment to find their current position and the next valley to the east. "It's about fifteen miles from here," she said.

"Where?" Ingrid asked.

"We are here, and the next one is there," Allie said as she placed a saltshaker on their current spot and the pepper shaker on where they needed to go next.

Without disturbing the shakers, Ingrid turned the map around so she could read it better. Once she had her bearings, she looked up the area on her phone and plunged in to locate any geocaches that might be in the area.

"You have a pen and paper on you? I left mine in the car."

Ingrid asked without looking up.

Allie dipped into her backpack and pulled out the requested items and slid them across the table. While she twisted in her seat, trying hard not to seem impatient, Allie looked out the window. The woman was gone and the man with the dog had made it only another twenty feet before stopping to chat with another man, also with a dog in tow. She checked in the other direction and saw no sign of her friends.

"I suppose any geocaches with a high terrain rating are out?" Ingrid asked.

"Let's try to stick to two or less. Preferably less," Allie answered.

Allie watched as Ingrid jotted down geocache ID numbers and coordinates for each. When she dropped the pen and sat back, there were four on the notepad.

"I think these are the most interesting. Especially the third one on the list," Ingrid said.

"What's so special about it?"

"The description says it's a petrified tree in the middle of nowhere."

"That does sound interesting. Should we go?" Allie said.

Ingrid nodded. "The only question that remains is whether to find Geneva and Drake and bring them along."

Allie dipped into her pocket and pulled out a euro coin. "The side with the man on it, we pick them up. The side with the number on it, we leave them here."

Allie flipped the coin high in the air, caught it on the way down, and slammed it onto the table. She smiled and removed her hand.

"Oh crap," Ingrid said when she saw the result.

*

"I can't believe you wanted to leave us behind," Geneva said, breaking almost a half hour of silence.

"Believe me, it wasn't us. It was the coin," Ingrid said. "It's pure good luck that you guys showed up when you did. Where did you disappear to, anyway?"

"We walked over to the church to check it out. It's beautiful inside. You should have seen the thing."

"Did you take lots of pictures?" Ingrid asked.

"Yes, I did. It was a beautiful church, wasn't it, honey?" Geneva asked. She elbowed Drake in the ribs when he didn't respond right away.

"Yes, dear. Beautiful church."

Allie caught Drake's eyes in the mirror, and when he rolled them, she couldn't suppress her smile.

"Wish I had been there," Allie said.

Luna told Allie to turn, and she did. After the turn, Allie drove another mile and parked in a small lot. The group emerged from the Fiat and stood in front of the car.

"That's not what I expected," Allie said. "I thought you said petrified tree."

"Yes, I did."

"I've visited the Petrified Forest in Arizona, and I've never seen a tree like that," Drake said.

"Me either," Geneva added.

Before the group stood a petrified tree unlike anything they'd ever experienced. The tree looked like a Saguaro cactus from the American southwest desert. The main trunk stood arrow straight and fifteen feet tall. Offshoots of branches, much thinner than the main trunk, spread out a few inches from the trunk and reached for the bright blue sky.

Geneva stopped to snap a picture while Ingrid brought up the cache description and looked for clues.

"The cache page says it's not on the tree, yet not far from it. Search for something similar, yet different," Ingrid said.

"How could you read that?" Drake asked. "Did you learn fluent Italian in the last couple of days?"

Ingrid smiled and held up her phone. "I didn't need to. The

cache owner has Italian and English descriptions on the page. It should be within ten feet of where we're standing."

The four spread out and looked for the geocache.

"There's a pile of rocks over here," Drake said as he pointed at the ground.

"I've got one here, too," Geneva said.

Ingrid was closest to Drake, so she decided to help him sort through his pile while Allie joined Geneva for hers.

"I really dislike these," Allie said, looking down at the fifty or sixty rocks that made up a tiny hill.

Geneva toed a rock and pushed it aside. "Yeah, me too. I usually skip these. Why don't we wait and see if they find it over there?"

Allie nodded. "That's a great idea. If they don't, we can ask for help here. Drake loves these things."

Geneva crouched and picked up a rock, looked underneath it, and placed it to the side. "We should at least pretend that we're looking hard for it."

Allie nodded, then picked up the rock closest to her. She examined it, found it to be an ordinary rock, and put it down. The second rock yielded nothing as well.

"Eureka!" Drake exclaimed.

Allie and Geneva looked over at Drake, where he held a small box above his head like he'd just pulled Excalibur from a stone. Allie dropped the rock she held, and she and Geneva joined the others.

Ingrid's phone rang, and she answered on the fourth ring. "Hello? Hold on, let me put you on speaker." Ingrid fumbled with the buttons and then nodded. "Okay. Go ahead."

"Hello, this is Victoria. Can you hear me?"

"Sure can," Allie said. "Go ahead."

"I translated what I could of the parchment you found today. There were some things I couldn't make out because the picture wasn't clear. If I had the parchment with me, I would have been able to do it all."

"Did you get anything helpful to our quest?" Allie asked.

"Oh, yes. If you go to the sixth valley, you'll find something that shouldn't exist in nature. Steadfast and still."

"You mean like, for example, a large, petrified tree in the middle of a field?" Drake said.

The line went silent.

"Did we lose her?" Geneva asked after a few seconds of no one speaking.

"No. I'm still here. A petrified tree would fit what's written here. How did you know that?"

"Because we're already here," Allie said.

"Oh. Well, then I would search that tree for the next clue if I were you," Victoria said.

"Okay. Thanks Victoria. I'll call you back if we need anything else," Ingrid said. She disconnected the call and stowed her phone.

As one, the group turned around and faced the tree. Allie stepped close to it and ran her hand along the surface. Although it looked smooth, she detected a complex texture beneath her fingertips. She marveled at the palette of colors, from the various hues of brown and gray to the stripes of yellow and orange, to the pink patches within.

"I can't believe Leonardo da Vinci hid a clue here. How would someone even do that with the technology available five hundred years ago?" Drake said.

"I don't know, but let's check it over anyway," Allie said. "Since the intertwined knots led me to the last clue, it would be a good bet that this one would be the same. Look for the knots."

Each person took a side of the tree and began the search.

"How high up should we look?" Geneva asked.

"I don't know," Allie said. "Start with anything at eye level and below. If we need to search higher, we'll figure it out."

Allie stood before the tree, three inches away. She scanned

the tree for marks, working her way from left to right. When she reached the far right, she dropped her gaze a few inches and searched the tree in the opposite direction. Allie followed the same pattern until she got close to the ground. When she couldn't look down any farther, she got to her knees, and eventually ended up on hands and knees, like she was a gardener picking weeds by hand.

"I got nothing," Allie said.

"Crawl over here and help me out, then," Ingrid said.

Allie moved forward and around the trunk. Ingrid stepped back two feet to make room for Allie.

"You make your way up, and I'll meet you in the middle," Ingrid said.

While Ingrid worked from the top-down, Allie scanned the tree from the bottom-up. Both women came up with the same results. Nothing.

Already close to the ground, Allie moved forward again, where Geneva was just about finished with her section.

"This is hopeless," Geneva said.

"Hey, I think I have something," Drake said. "Allie, crawl on over here and take a look."

Allie did as requested and moved around to Drake's side of the tree. There, he pointed at something near where the trunk met the ground. Allie strained to see and then touched the spot.

"I don't think that's anything," Allie said.

"No. Go lower, where that little nub comes out of the ground."

Allie found the spot Drake alluded to. Nub was the correct term, as it looked like someone had dropped a rock the size of a plum on the ground. She leaned over to check it out, and sure enough, peeking out above the grass, was the top half of the intertwined knots they'd been searching for.

"Can you find me a stick or something to dig with?" Allie asked.

Geneva, Drake, and Ingrid scoured the area, and together they found two flat rocks, a stick, and a plastic spoon. Allie looked at the options available and selected the spoon from Drake's hand. She went to work on the grass around the nub and uncovered it one spoonful at a time. The nub turned out to be the part of an exposed petrified root from the tree. Allie dug out as much as she could until the entirety of the knots symbol was clear of dirt and debris. Unlike the one from earlier in the day, this one didn't have a hole in the center. Allie pushed on the knots, and nothing happened.

"I don't understand," Allie said. "When I put pressure on the last one, the hole opened."

"Maybe you need to dig down farther. It could be it's underneath the tree," Drake said.

"Well, then grab something and get down here and help me."

Drake looked at the items available to him and selected a rock in the shape of an arrowhead and the stick. He moved to the side opposite Allie and began to dig with the rock, pushing the dirt to the side as he released it.

"You need more help down there?" Geneva asked.

"Yes, but there's not really any room for you. Why don't y'all take a break, and when one of us gets tired, you can take our place," Allie said.

Geneva nodded and stayed standing where she was. Ingrid moved a few feet away and sat cross-legged on the grass, watching as Allie and Drake worked to uncover the root.

Everyone stayed silent as Drake and Allie pawed at the dirt. As if a cruel joke, a cool wind blew through the valley, and off in the distance, a peal of rumble echoed through the mountains.

"My guess is you guys should dig a little faster," Geneva said.

Drake stopped, looked at the sky, and then back at Geneva. "Maybe it's time for you guys to jump in and help. I'd hate to do this in the rain."

Ingrid kneeled next to Allie and Geneva crowded in beside Drake and four hands working on the single task became eight.

The thunder rumbled again, and the sky darkened as more storm clouds rolled in.

The four quickly got into a rhythm, with Allie and Drake loosening the dirt while Ingrid and Geneva pushed it aside. After ten minutes, Allie reached under the root and touched Drake's fingertips.

"We're through. We need to expand the hole," Allie said.

The group redoubled the effort, and soon the hole doubled, then quadrupled in size.

"Hold on, I think I have something. Someone give me a phone," Allie said as she rubbed the underside of the root.

"Here," Ingrid said, passing her phone to Allie.

Allie took the phone, set the camera to rear-facing, and moved it under the root. There, plain as day, she saw another set of intertwined knots on the screen. Like the previous find, this set had a hole in the center.

"Pass me that stick, Drake," Allie said.

Drake gave up the wood, and realizing it was too long to fit, Allie broke the stick in half. She placed the stick under the root, used her index finger to guide her over the hole, then inserted the stick and pushed. When she felt resistance, she pushed harder, and a chunk of the tree dropped into her hand.

Allie pulled the stick and tree from the hole, then without looking, reached underneath into the hole.

"I got something. Feels like a string or something," Allie said.

Allie caught the item between two fingers and pulled. A leather strap dropped from the hole, so Allie wrapped her fingers around it and gave it a hearty yank. She spotted the edge of a parchment and eventually wiggled it free.

"Got it," Allie said, holding the find in the air. As soon as she finished speaking, the first of the big, lazy raindrops began plopping to the ground.

"I guess it's time to get going," Ingrid said as she got to her feet.

"Let's cover this back up first," Drake said.

As one, they pushed the dirt into the hole until they'd covered even the nub, and then Drake took some time and set the disrupted grass back in place. Once everything looked as natural as could be, the four friends jogged back to the car.

Once they all entered the Fiat and closed the doors, Allie fired up the engine just as a flash of lightning streaked across the sky.

"It really is time to go," Allie said. She put the car into gear, did a U-turn in the small parking area, and headed for the road.

"Are you going to send Victoria a picture of this new parchment?" Allie had the parchment on the seat next to her, and Ingrid leaned over and grabbed it.

Ingrid unrolled the parchment, propped it up against the glove compartment and snapped a picture. She opened her texts, then realized she had a problem. "I can't do it. I lost service," she said.

"Must be the storm," Geneva said from the back.

As they drove on, the rain grew harder, forcing Allie to slow down and set the windshield wipers on high.

"How far is town?" Allie asked.

"Only three or four miles," Ingrid said.

"Okay. If this rain doesn't let up by then, I'm going to pull in somewhere until it eases. I have no desire to drive four hours through this downpour."

As Allie stopped speaking, she noticed the windshield had started to fog.

"Ingrid, can you mess with the fan and clear that out?"

Ingrid flipped on the defroster, and as she did, a gust of wind came through the valley like an oncoming train. It caught

Allie off guard, and it pushed the Fiat into the oncoming lane until Allie regained control and navigated back where she belonged. The rain picked up, and Allie slowed even further, unable to see only three feet beyond the hood. She took her hand off the steering wheel just long enough to flip on the hazard lights and struggled to keep the car on the pavement. She hadn't realized she'd been holding her breath until she passed the village limits sign. Allie exhaled, flexed her hands over the steering wheel, and pulled into the first parking lot she came to.

# CHAPTER EIGHTEEN

"Allie?"

Allie opened her eyes and noticed Ingrid's perfect face in front of hers.

"Good morning," Ingrid said.

Allie smiled. "Good morning. What's up?"

"Everything but you. Drake wants to know what the plan is for today. Are we going to the seventh valley?"

"Yes. What time is it?"

Ingrid checked. "It's a bit after nine. I hated waking you. I can't imagine how tired you are."

Allie nodded and closed her eyes. Tired was an understatement. The day before, they'd waited in the parking lot for an hour for the rain to let up, and when it didn't, they returned to the restaurant to hunker down somewhere warmer and more comfortable than the car. The sunset took the rain with it, and only afterward did they begin the four-hour drive back to the hotel.

"Allie?"

"No, I'm getting up right now." Allie threw the blanket off

and managed to swing her legs over the edge of the bed.

"Would you like some tea?" Ingrid asked.

"I'd love a cup. I'll be down to the dining room in ten minutes." Allie rubbed her eyes and ran her fingers through her tangled hair. "Actually, I'd love a shower, too, so I'll be down in fifteen."

"Here," Ingrid said.

Allie accepted what Ingrid handed her without question. It was a mug, steam coming off the top. Allie sniffed.

"Is this cinnamon?" Allie asked.

Ingrid nodded. "Yep. With a dollop of honey, the way you like it."

Allie smiled and took a sip. "This is wonderful. I love you so much right now."

Ingrid grinned. "How could you not? I'm adorable. I'll catch you downstairs in a bit."

Sixteen minutes later, Allie strolled into the dining room. Her hair was still wet from the shower, and she'd revived the bounce in her step. "Good morning, everyone," she said as she placed her empty mug on the table. "What's good for breakfast today?"

"The sandwiches aren't bad," Drake said.

For breakfast, the hotel laid out a variety of meats, breads, and cheeses, in addition to the common breakfast fare. Rather than go for the cereal or oatmeal, Drake had taken to making sandwiches instead, usually salami, ham, and cheese between thick slices of fresh-baked Italian bread.

"Did you send the picture off to Victoria for translation?" Allie asked Ingrid.

"Yep, I did that first thing. She reached out and asked for closeups and additional shots of some things, so I sent those off too. She should get back to us within the hour."

"Do you guys mind if I eat something before we head out?"

Drake pointed toward the food. "Go ahead. I highly

recommend the salami stuff and that white cheese."

Allie headed over to the breakfast bar, made herself a plate, and returned to the table. She put her plate on the table and slid into a chair next to Ingrid.

"This will be the seventh valley. Perhaps this is the day we get to the end of the mystery," Allie said.

"It would be nice," Geneva said. "Not so much from the standpoint of becoming rich and famous, but more like getting back to our normally scheduled vacation."

"Is all the driving getting to you?" Drake asked.

Geneva thought for a moment, finishing a corner of toast before she answered. "It's not that. I enjoy the adventure, and don't mind the rides. I'd simply like to get more immersed in the culture. Visit more of the city sites? You get what I'm saying."

Allie nodded. "I do. I was hoping to get a few museums in, and we haven't stepped inside a single one."

"And I won't. I'll wait outside, or do something else," Drake said.

"We've got another ten days here. Why don't we take the day off and do something else?" Ingrid asked.

Allie pointed her oatmeal spoon in Ingrid's direction. "That's a good idea. We could all split up for the day, do our own things. Have a down day. If there is a hidden pile of artifacts out there, they've been there for five hundred years. Another day won't change that. We can go to the valley tomorrow. Or the day after, or whenever."

Geneva sat fiddling with a spoon. "No. I think we should go for it today. I'm sure it's on all our minds, so we get it out of the way. And then we return to the scheduled programming."

"Are you sure, honey?" Drake asked.

"Yes. Let's do it and get it out of the way," Geneva said.

"That's it then. We'll go for it as soon as we get the translation back from Victoria," Allie said.

Everyone had finished breakfast and Allie barely finished

her third mug of cinnamon tea when Ingrid received the call they'd been waiting for. She jotted down the information and closed out the call.

"The parchment leads to the seventh valley, like we all assumed. There, beneath the tallest peak, we'll find what we've been looking for," Ingrid said.

"I don't like the idea of being under the tallest peak," Drake said. "Does that mean at the mountaintop? Or at the base?"

"We won't know until we get there," Allie said. "Y'all get your stuff, and I'll go get the car. Ingrid, can you grab my backpack? I think I left it on the chair next to the window."

"Sure thing."

"Okay, then. I'll be back in five minutes," Allie said.

Twenty minutes later, Allie returned to the hotel on foot to find her friends standing outside the hotel waiting for her.

"Where's the car?" Drake asked.

"Won't start," Allie said.

"For real?"

"No, Drake. Not for real. I spent the last half hour waiting around the corner to play a practical joke on you. So, the laughs are on you! Of course, it's real. The starter clicks when I turn the key, but it won't turn over."

"What's wrong with it?" Ingrid asked.

"I don't know."

"Did you check under the hood?" Geneva asked.

"Okay," Allie said, holding up her hands in defense. "Everyone come with me."

Allie turned around and led the group away from the hotel. Together, they walked in the bright morning sun three blocks to a public parking garage. Rather than wait for the old, slow elevator, Allie guided them up a flight of steps to the first floor, and walked halfway across the garage. There, the Fiat sat in its spot, right where they'd left it the night before.

"Okay, pop the hood," Drake said.

"Drake, you know nothing about cars. What good is popping the hood going to do?" Allie asked.

"It's something they always do on television. Just do it. I had a problem once where I thought I was having major car trouble, and I took it in and found that my battery cables were loose. I admit I'm not exactly a mechanic, but even I can wiggle a cable to check if it's loose."

Allie unlocked the doors, opened hers, and leaned in and activated the hood release. Drake opened the hood and set the strut in place to hold it open. He dipped his head over the engine, then looked around to the side of the car where the three women waited for his report.

"I found the problem," Drake said.

"Loose cable?" Geneva asked.

"You might say that. Come and take a look."

Drake stepped aside to make room for everyone else. The women lined up in front of the engine compartment and looked in.

"Yeah, I can tell where the problem is," Allie said. "Son of a bitch. Who? Why?"

Inside the engine compartment, someone had sliced clean in half every accessible hose and wire.

"How does something like that happen?" Ingrid asked.

"I know. I've heard of catalytic converters being ripped off a car, but this is way beyond that," Drake said. "It doesn't even look like anything is missing, just vandalized."

"So, what do we do now?" Geneva asked.

"Head back to our hotel, call the rental car place, and hope I get someone who speaks really good English," Allie said.

"You seem remarkably composed about this," Drake said. "I'm not sure I'd be the same way if something like this happened to my truck."

Allie shrugged. "It's not my car. And I got the full additional insurance package. I guess this time it was well worth the extra money. Step back."

Once her friends moved aside, Allie released the strut, tucked it back into place, and slammed the hood shut. Silently, she led the group from the parking structure and returned to the hotel. Allie stopped at the desk and her friends continued to the breakfast area.

"What did they say?" Geneva asked when Allie returned. She looked around the table, everyone was waiting for her response with interest.

"Well, thanks to the front desk clerk who helped translate our situation, the rental company will send us a replacement car and pick this one up," Allie said.

"That's it?" Drake asked.

"Yep. We should get it sometime this afternoon."

"Another problem solved," Geneva said.

"And we get a little downtime you wanted," Ingrid said. "What should we do with the day?"

"I wouldn't mind returning to that big park we visited a few days ago. The one by the water. There are a few other monuments I wouldn't mind seeing, and they have the Volta Museum I'd like to walk though," Allie said.

"Who's Volta?" Drake asked.

"He invented the electric battery," Allie said.

"And you want to go to that museum because?"

"Because, unlike you, Drake Decker, I have an appreciation for history."

"What do you want to do?" Drake asked Geneva.

"I'm not sure. Walk around, maybe visit a few shops. Maybe we can check about getting a replacement phone for you."

"That's actually an excellent idea. I propose a free day. Geneva and I will hit the shops, and you two can do what you two do," Drake said.

Allie nodded. "That works for me. Ingrid, would you prefer to go shopping with them or hang with me?"

Ingrid looked from Allie to Geneva. "I'm not big on shopping, so I'll come with you. Although I may wait outside the museum for you if I decide to pass."

"Okay. That's a deal," Allie said. "I'll give Geneva a call later this afternoon and we'll discuss what we want to do about dinner."

"Great," Drake said. "I guess until later, then. Enjoy your day."

Allie and Ingrid watched as the couple took their leave and headed toward the front door.

"You ready?" Allie asked.

"Let me go dump my backpack in the room first. I don't want to haul it around all day," Ingrid said.

"Good idea. I'll come with you. I don't feel like carrying around anything I don't need to today. Why lug it if you don't need it, right?"

An hour later, Ingrid and Allie were walking along the waterfront, hand in hand. Off in the distance, the Volta Museum stood visible, its neoclassical style and four stately columns on display.

"Are you upset we didn't go to the valley today?" Ingrid asked.

"No. Not for a minute," Allie said. "Look at us. Enjoying a gorgeous day and taking it easy for a change. Regardless of what y'all think, sometimes I like a slower pace. This stuff isn't too boring for you, is it?"

"Of course not. I enjoy taking in the history just like you do."

They stopped when they got in front of the museum.

"Are you coming in with me?" Allie asked.

Ingrid let loose a deep exhale.

Allie laughed. "Just say no, sweetheart. It's fine. We're not joined at the hip or anything. Besides, you'd be more help to me if you did me a favor while I'm in there."

"Sure. What?"

Allie pointed at a park bench off to the side of the museum next to the water. "You see that bench over there? Can you go grab that bench, so I have a place to sit down when I'm done exploring inside the building?"

"That, I can do." Ingrid said.

The women parted ways, and Allie watched as Ingrid headed for the bench. She took a moment to snap a picture of the building, then headed for the door. Once she paid her admission fee, Allie stepped into the rotunda of the building and spun in a circle, marveling at the marble columns and floor. Each direction led to an alcove featuring an original invention or other aspect of Alessandro Volta's life and career.

Allie took her time exploring the exhibits, and after a while she ended up back at the first exhibit she viewed. She glanced at her phone, and it shocked her to see that she'd spent just over an hour inside the space.

She rushed outside, working on her apology to Ingrid for taking so long, turned the corner, and where she expected to spot only Ingrid waiting for her on the bench, she noticed the backs of two heads instead. Allie picked up her pace and rounded the bench. There, sitting on the opposite side of the bench Ingrid, was Lorenzo.

"I'm so sorry I took so long, Ingrid," Allie said when Ingrid noticed her.

"Don't worry about it. I know how you get lost in those things. Besides, Lorenzo's been keeping me company."

"Lorenzo," Allie said. "Nice to see you again." Allie put out her hand for Lorenzo to shake, but Lorenzo got to his feet and kissed both of Allie's cheeks in a traditional greeting.

"Please, sit next to your friend," Lorenzo said, offering his seat to Allie. "Ingrid said you were inside the museum? Some fascinating things in there."

"There are," Allie agreed. "What are you doing here?"

"I live near to here, so I always walk along the lakefront and through the park. I'm here usually five days a week. While on my journey today, I spotted Ingrid sitting along, and I stopped to say hello, and she invited me to sit with her until you returned."

"Thank you for keeping her company while I was away," Allie said. "Ingrid—"

"Lorenzo was telling me about his life and desire to visit America," Ingrid said, interrupting.

"You've never been to America?" Allie asked.

"No, but it's always been my dream to visit. Tell me, where do you two come from?"

"Well," Allie said, "I'm from Nashville, and Ingrid is from Boston."

"Nashville and Boston? Those are by New York City?" Lorenzo asked.

"No. I'm about four hours away from New York by car," Ingrid said.

"And I'm about fourteen hours away," Allie said.

"Fourteen hours? By auto? That is like going from here to London."

"The United States is a big country," Allie said.

"If Ingrid is four hours away and you are fourteen, then you don't live near each other?"

"No," Allie said. "I'm more from the middle of the country. Do you know of any cities in the middle?"

"Like Chicago?"

"Yes. Exactly. My city is about five hundred miles south of Chicago."

"And so then, where is Los Angeles?"

Allie thought for a second. "L.A. is roughly two thousand miles to the west of me."

"Two thousand miles? How many kilometers is that?" Lorenzo asked.

"It would be like going from here to Minsk," Ingrid said. "From my home to L.A. is like going from Rome to Moscow."

Lorenzo's jaw dropped. "That far? In one country?"

Ingrid laughed. "Yes. The United States is large. You could spend a year there and not see everything there is to see."

"I would like to try," Lorenzo said. "I would like to see the entire world."

"You live in Europe. There isn't enough to see here?" Ingrid said. "There are so many places I would visit if I lived here. I'd love to see France, Germany, Spain. I've been here before, but only to England and Scandinavia."

"Bah. I've traveled around here, and I'm ready to leave. I'd like to visit everywhere. Africa, Australia, China, Brazil. Anywhere but here," Lorenzo said.

"But you said it was your dream to study. What was it, Hannibal?" Ingrid said.

"Actually, that was more my father's dream than mine. Since I was a boy, he told me stories about Hannibal and his great journey across the mountains. And I admit, I grew fascinated by those stories early on, but the more I studied them, the less they appealed to me."

"So, what do you want?" Ingrid asked.

"Like I said. I want to see the world for myself, not just learn about it in some classroom or dusty old library. Even this museum, as beautiful and historic as it is, isn't for me. I'd die if I had to spend my entire life inside one like my father wants."

"What does your father do now?" Allie asked.

"He's a merchant. Selling goods to the locals and trinkets to the tourists. He dreams of a better life for me, but I think he secretly dreams that if I had the money, I would help him get by and he could close his shop for good. That's another reason I'd like to go to America."

"Why?"

"So that I could be rich, of course. You're rich, aren't you?"

Ingrid and Allie looked into each other's eyes, an unsaid understanding growing between them not to say anything about finances.

"The idea that all Americans are rich is only a story. Most of us live paycheck to paycheck or work multiple jobs just to make ends meet," Ingrid said. "The big houses and lavish lifestyles you see in the movies or on television shows only show a small percentage of how most Americans really live. Unlike what you've heard, the streets aren't really paved with gold."

"But there are wealthy people there, right?" Lorenzo asked.

"Yes. Just like most everywhere," Allie said.

"I would take my chances there, where I could do anything, or be anything I wanted to be. Make a fortune several times over."

Allie prepared to deliver a response when she got literally saved by the bell, in this case her phone ring tone.

"I'm sorry, I need to get this," Allie said as she reached for the answer button. "Hello? Yes, this is she. Okay, how long? Right. See you then." Allie disconnected the phone and turned to Ingrid. "That was the rental company. I need to get back to the car so we can swap it out."

Ingrid nodded and stood without saying anything.

"I'm sorry, Lorenzo, but we need to go. It's been a pleasure speaking with you," Allie said. She reached out for Ingrid's hand, then pulled her into a swift walk.

Ingrid turned and waved goodbye.

"What's he doing?" Allie asked.

"Staring at us," Ingrid said.

"What's the level on your creepy mete?"

"Out of ten? Twelve. Let's walk a little faster."

# CHAPTER NINETEEN

At fourteen minutes after eleven the next morning, Allie drove the replacement Fiat into the seventh valley. Unlike the other valleys, this one contained no towns, shops, houses, or people. It was also the smallest valley by far. A river ran through the middle, and other than the two-lane road that followed the banks, each side of the river measured at most two hundred yards before the slopes climbed into mountaintops.

Alongside the road were pullouts every few hundred yards that offered spots for fishermen and others to park, but as they traveled through the valley, all the parking areas were empty.

The day before, Allie and Geneva had worked out which peak along the four-mile-long valley was the tallest and determined it was the one at the farthest end.

"I think this is the most beautiful one yet," Geneva said as she stared out the window, watching the natural wonder pass by.

"Me too. I like the spooky, claustrophobic vibe of it," Ingrid said.

"You would," Geneva said. "How long until we get there?"

Allie snuck a peek at Luna. "Couple of minutes yet. We're

almost there."

"I hope there's a place to park," Drake said.

"If there's not, we can take the next closest spot and hike in," Allie said.

Allie smiled when Drake let out a groan that filled the entire car for everyone to enjoy.

"It'll be fine. If there's no spot there, I can drop the three of you off and park the car and hike back myself."

"How is it you're the one with the busted-up knee, yet you're the one having to do all the hard walks on this trip?" Drake asked.

"I'm not the only one with an excuse anymore. You, Geneva, and Ingrid are all injured, too."

"Actually, I'm like my old self. I completely forgot about twisting my ankle," Geneva said.

"I'm fine, too," Ingrid added. "You know, I think even the few scars I had are starting to fade."

"What I'm hearing is Drake is the only one here with a problem?" Allie teased. "Any objections to dropping him off and hiking in ourselves?"

"I'm down for it," Ingrid said.

"Me, too. It would be nice to have some girl time," Geneva added.

"We're only a few hundred yards away," Allie said. "Hold on to those hopes."

Allie slowed down as they reached the destination and pulled into an area that seemed large enough to fit three cars. Once they were out into the open, Ingrid found a path that led across the road to the river, and Geneva found one that headed up the slope toward the mountain peak.

"I guess we go this way," Geneva said, pointing up the path.

"Lead the way," Allie said.

Geneva took point and led the group along the narrow path that climbed straight up the slope for ten feet, then started a steep ascent diagonally across the hill. They trudged on one stride at a time. After fifteen minutes, Geneva stopped, turned around, and looked at the group behind her. Each of them was breathing heavily, and although it was a cool day, Drake, unlike the rest of them, had beads of sweat sliding down his forehead.

"Why did you stop?" Ingrid asked.

"Because the trail did," Geneva said. "Check it out."

Ingrid was next in line and was facing Geneva. She leaned to her left and saw that the trail ended at the sheer side of the mountain.

"There's nowhere to go?" Ingrid asked.

Geneva turned back around and studied her options. "Well, there are two. If you can climb a wall, you can go up, and if you want to fall, you can take a step to your right and slide down to the car."

"There's no entrance there?" Allie asked from the back.

"Not one that's readily apparent. You're welcome to come up here and look."

"Okay, I will."

Drake had a large flat rock to his right big enough to accommodate him, so he stepped onto that and let Allie take his spot in line. Then he stepped off and walked down the trail a few feet to make room for Ingrid and Geneva. By using the same technique Drake did, Ingrid and Geneva took turns stepping on his rock to allow Allie to move to the front of the line.

Once she faced the mountain, Allie got a better idea of what Geneva described. Directly in front of her, the trail ended at the face. To her left was the mountain, and to her right, the mountain dropped away. Allie scanned the surface for Leonardo's knots, but after a futile search, she had to admit to herself that there was nothing to be found.

She turned around and faced her friends. "There's nothing here."

"That's what I said," Geneva said. "What should we do?"

"Head back down, I guess," Allie said.

Drake led the group back down the path and to the car. When they got to the parking area, they spotted an ancient pickup truck that displayed so much rust it was hard to determine if the original color was brown or red.

Allie unlocked the back of the Fiat, and from a shopping bag, retrieved four bottles of water. She passed them out to everyone, then sat on the SUV's bumper and took a deep drink.

"I'm sorry, you guys. I thought for sure it would be up there," Allie said.

"It's not your fault," Drake said. "We're playing a five-century game here. It would be foolish to expect that everything would work out."

"Perhaps the translation was wrong somehow," Ingrid said. "I'll give Victoria a call." Ingrid made an attempt, but the call didn't go through.

"What now?" Drake asked.

"We head back. Return to our geocaching and touring." Allie said.

"It's a shame. I like it here," Ingrid said. "Do you mind if I take a few pictures before we go?"

Allie shrugged. "Knock yourself out. We're in no hurry."

Ingrid grinned like a child being offered an ice cream cone, then checked the road for traffic and headed to the path leading to the river. Allie watched as Ingrid plodded down the path, then turned left and disappeared down the bank. She had another drink of water and shifted her butt to get comfortable while waiting for her friend. She heard a door open, then felt someone sit in the car.

"What's going on up there?" Allie asked.

"We're having sex!" Drake yelled, a note of triumph in his voice.

Geneva let loose a loud sigh. "We are not. I'm taking a stone out of my shoe."

"Is that what they're calling it these days?" Allie said. She laughed, and Drake joined her.

"That's not funny," Geneva said.

Drake stepped to the rear of the van and faced Allie. "She didn't like that."

"Are you okay? You're sweating up a storm."

Drake wiped his forehead with his hand, then looked at his glistening palm. "I guess so."

"Sit down here. Drink some water," Allie said. She jumped off the bumper and Drake took her place.

Drake unscrewed the cap from his water and lifted the bottle to his lips. He hesitated for the briefest of seconds, then his eyes rolled back into his head, and he fell forward and landed face down in the dirt.

"Oh, shit, Drake!" Allie yelled. She dropped to her knees beside her fallen friend.

"What happened?" Geneva asked when she got to the scene.

"He fainted. Can you call for help? Drake? Can you hear me?"

Allie checked for his pulse in his neck, then in his arm. She dropped her ear to near his mouth. "He's got a pulse, and he's breathing. I don't know what the problem is. Did you get through?"

"No," Geneva said.

"Help me get him in the car."

Allie got under one of Drake's arms, and Geneva got the other one, and together they struggled to get Drake into the back seat of the Fiat. Geneva got into the backseat with Drake and rested his head on her lap.

"Okay, let's go," Allie said, opening the driver's door.

"No! You forgot Ingrid," Geneva yelled.

"Oh, shit. Don't tell her. I'll be right back."

Allie left the car, ran across the road without looking, and jogged down the only path available to her. She ran without observing her environment, and at one point kicked a rock and sprawled to the ground. She jumped up without brushing herself off and picked up her pace.

The path followed the river and bent inward toward the mountain. Allie didn't even realize she'd entered a cave until she'd taken four strides inside and slid to a stop when she found Ingrid standing still right before her.

Allie reached out for Ingrid's hand. "Come on. Drake's sick. We need to go right now."

Ingrid didn't move or speak. Allie looked into her eyes and saw a look of concern that she guessed wasn't for Drake alone. She watched as Ingrid slowly lifted her chin.

Allie pivoted to face the cave entrance and stopped. Lorenzo blocked the way, holding a shotgun.

"What is this?" Allie asked.

"A stick-up," Lorenzo sneered. "You don't think I knew what you were looking for? I could tell the second I spotted that scroll."

"You said you couldn't read the old Italian on there," Allie said.

"I lied. I knew if I got someone else to help you, I could follow you without you suspecting me."

"What do you want from us?" Allie asked.

"The treasure, of course. My father didn't tell me stories only of Hannibal crossing the Alps. He also told me the legends of the lost treasure of Leonardo."

"Look, we have to go," Allie growled. "Our friend is sick."

Allie took a step toward Lorenzo, and he responded by holding out the shotgun.

"I will shoot if you move again. Put your hands up."

Allie and Ingrid both complied.

"What are you going to do with us?" Ingrid asked.

"First thing I'm going to do is have you explore this cave for me and find the treasure. After that, who's to say? Get going."

Allie and Ingrid turned around and faced the inner cave.

"It's dark in there. We'll never be able to find anything," Allie said.

Allie detected two thunks at her feet and turned around. There, she spotted two flashlights. She picked them up, turned one on, and handed the other to Ingrid.

"Happy?" Lorenzo asked. "Go on."

Allie swept the light through the cave. At most it was eight feet deep, but she saw a black hand-painted arrow on the back wall that pointed to the left. She walked in that direction with Ingrid right on her heels and Lorenzo two yards behind Ingrid.

Allie followed the arrows deeper into the cave. Not that she needed to, since there was only one way to go. There were no alternate branches to explore at all, so she moved as quickly as she dared, hoping to find a way to ditch Lorenzo and get back to Drake. Allie noticed the temperature drop at first as they ventured deeper into the labyrinth, and then it evened out.

"How far should I go?" Allie asked.

"As far as it takes. Keep moving. Don't stop."

Allie continued following the black arrows and eventually they led to a large cavern the size of an ice rink. Stalactites and stalagmites added an ambiance that other circumstances would have been quite enjoyable, but instead they added a dreary, damp feel.

"Ingrid, stop," Lorenzo said. "Your friend stays with me. You check around here and let me know what you find. You come back empty-handed, and Ingrid will have a problem."

Allie nodded that she understood, then stepped farther into the cavern. She found the sweet spot where the light would reach the walls, yet she could stay closer to the center of the room and navigate the rock formations. She got a quarter way around the room when she got to an area where the stalagmites were a few feet offset from the wall, forming a gap not easily noticed.

Inside the gap sat two large chests, not unlike the type Allie had seen in countless pirate movies. She opened the one closest to her and shined the flashlight inside. Empty. Allie opened the next one and this time the light found a large leather satchel covered in dust. She opened the bag, and from within withdrew a journal made of parchment, covered in leather. When she shined the light on the pages, she recognized hand-drawn blueprints similar to those associated with Leonardo da Vinci. Allie turned page after page, then set the journal down and extracted another from the satchel. Satisfied she'd found the treasure, she stowed everything away and closed both chests.

Now that she had what she needed, Allie continued her way around the cavern, looking for something to use as a weapon. She stopped briefly to check something that caught her eye, but since it was neither a weapon nor a way out, she continued her journey around the room. When she completed the circle, she stepped in front of Lorenzo.

"It's back there," Allie said, shining the light in the general direction of the chests.

"Go. Show me," Lorenzo ordered.

Allie led the way, and when they arrived at the chests, Lorenzo pushed the women against the wall, and while keeping one eye on them, opened both chests. Like Allie had done, Lorenzo extracted a journal from the satchel and opened it. As he did, he lowered the shotgun slightly and Allie took a hesitant step forward.

"No," Lorenzo said, returning the shotgun to chest height. Keeping the women in his sights, Lorenzo removed a bag from his shoulder and tossed it to Ingrid. "There's rope in there. Tie up your friend."

Ingrid didn't move. Lorenzo stepped forward and placed the barrel of the shotgun on Allie's forehead.

"Tie her or lose her. Your choice."

"Okay, okay," Ingrid said, bending over to find the rope. When she found it, she bound Allie's wrists behind her back as directed, and then secured Allie to a nearby stalagmite. Once Ingrid tied up Allie tight, Lorenzo tied Ingrid to Allie. Once he trussed up the women, Lorenzo turned his full attention to the chests.

"This discovery will make me rich beyond comprehension," Lorenzo said as he cleared items from the chest.

"Take the treasure, let us go," Allie said.

"Oh, no, I can't do that. You'll tell the authorities. Did you look in here? Journals. Art. Gold. No. You'll need to stay right where you are."

"Our friends will come and find us," Ingrid said.

Her comment gave Lorenzo pause, and he dropped the gold coins he had in his hand back into the chest.

"Yes. The other two. I'll deal with them as well. I thank you for the reminder. Now, if you'll excuse me, I'll go tend to them."

Lorenzo took a moment to shove as many items from the chest as he could fit into his shoulder bag. Then he did the same with two satchels from the chest. Confident he couldn't carry any more, he took Ingrid's flashlight, turned it off, and put it into his pocket. Allie's flashlight he picked up and left the cavern, leaving Allie and Ingrid in the pitch black.

Neither woman spoke, and in the quiet somewhere, Allie heard a drop of water fall into a puddle, followed thirty seconds later by another.

"How are we going to get out of this one?" Ingrid asked.

"I was just thinking about that very thing. I don't suppose calling for help will do any good."

"Probably not. You don't happen to have a knife in your pocket, do you?"

"No," Allie said. "Even if I did, it wouldn't do much good since I can't reach my pocket. You tied me too tight."

"Sorry. I thought he would check it."

"He did. You did the right thing. Can you move at all?"

Allie felt Ingrid make an attempt, but she could tell Ingrid struggled against her bonds.

"Not much," Ingrid said. "Maybe if we worked together, we could break this rock thing and get some slack."

Allie counted to three, and despite their best efforts, they didn't move more than a half inch.

"I think he's coming back," Allie said. "I can see light coming this way."

"Can we kick him or something?" Ingrid asked.

"I can't move my legs," Allie said.

The light got closer, and when it was within three feet, it shined directly into their faces.

"You're still here. Good," Lorenzo said. "One more trip, I think, and then I can take care of your friends."

The light moved from the women to the chest, and once again Lorenzo filled his bag and the three remaining satchels from the chest. When he finished, he shined the light into the bottom of both chests. Then he tipped over a chest and checked for a false compartment, and finding none, repeated the action with the remaining chest.

"And now, I'll say goodbye for now. Don't worry, though. I'll be back within twenty or thirty minutes to let you go."

The light turned and grew smaller as Lorenzo left the cavern.

"You really believe he's going to let us go?" Ingrid asked.

"Not a chance. We need to escape from here. Let's try moving back and forth and see if that helps. Maybe we can press the rope against the rock and cut through it," Allie said.

Since Ingrid's hands were in front, she could make sure part of her rope contacted the stalagmite, and together, they produced a slight rocking motion, moving side to side an inch at a time. For what seemed like hours, they worked in silence trying to break their bonds. The rope held.

"He's coming back," Allie said, noticing the light dancing toward them.

"Great," Ingrid said. "I guess this is it. Going out trapped like this was something I never envisioned for myself. I had hoped to die in bed as an old woman, with my great-great-great grandchildren at my side."

"Shh, he's almost here."

The light stopped a few feet from them and hung still, illuminating the faces of Ingrid and Allie.

"So do you gals want to leave here, or what?" Geneva asked from behind the light.

# CHAPTER TWENTY

"Allie, do you have any threes?" Ingrid asked.

"Crap. Here." Allie passed the three of diamonds to Ingrid, who paired it with the three of spades in her hand and placed them on the table in front of her.

"I'm telling you, she's an expert at this game. She could go pro," Geneva said.

"What game?" Drake asked.

The women stopped their game and looked over toward the bed.

"Go, Fish," Geneva said as she stood and moved to Drake's bedside. "How are you feeling?"

"Tired. What happened?"

"When you had surgery, they didn't get all the wood out of your stomach, so you got an infection. They had to operate on you again."

"Am I better?" Drake asked.

Geneva brought his hand to her lips and kissed his fingers. "Yes, thankfully. You had us all scared."

"How long have I been here?"

"Three days. You've been sleeping a lot, though. Don't you remember anything from recently?"

Drake shook his head no. Near his bed was a large cup of water. He reached for it, and Geneva held it steady while he drank.

"I suppose we should catch you up. What's the last thing you remember?"

"We climbed up and down that mountain, and you wanted to have sex in the car," Drake said.

"Close enough. Well, in a nutshell, you passed out. Allie and Ingrid got kidnapped, I caught the culprit, and Allie discovered Leonardo da Vinci's hidden stockpile."

Drake struggled to sit up, so Geneva found the controls and lifted the bed's head until he reached a comfortable position.

"Perhaps instead of only the nutshell, you should give me the whole nut."

"Okay. You passed out, so Allie and I got you into the car. Allie was ready to race you back to civilization when I realized we were about to leave Ingrid behind."

"Wait, really? You were going to leave me there?" Ingrid said, dropping the cards in her hand onto the table.

"No, of course not, honey," Allie said. "We would have come back for you, eventually."

Ingrid made a face of mock anger and waved her fist in the air.

"Calm down, you two," Geneva scolded. "Anyway, we noticed Ingrid was still missing, so Allie decided to look for her. She was gone for a long time, so I headed out to search for both of them. I followed the path that ran along the river and had just stepped around the bend when I saw Lorenzo bent over, emptying bags of something on the ground. When he disappeared back into the cave, I ran over and discovered that he had all kinds of interesting things."

"Why didn't you come for us?" Ingrid asked.

"I tried to, but I only made it like three feet into the cave until it got too dark, and I didn't have a flashlight on me. I also saw Lorenzo had a rifle on him, so I didn't want to get too close to him."

"Valid points," Ingrid conceded.

"Then what?" Drake asked.

"Then I rushed back to our back to our car. I considered driving for help, since the keys were dangling from the ignition, but I didn't want to leave you guys. I assumed Lorenzo was the one who disabled our other car, so I wanted to return the favor."

"That was probably a good assumption," Allie said. "He followed us for days, apparently. Must be good at it, too, because I never spotted him."

"Me neither," Ingrid said.

"What did you do? Cut all his wires?" Drake asked.

"I thought about it, but I had nothing to cut with. I got the tire iron from our trunk and used it like a pry bar to dislodge a few things in his engine. Even though I didn't know what I was doing. I just figured if I could disconnect something, anything, then he'd be stuck there," Geneva said.

"So, you wanted the guy with the gun there with us?" Ingrid asked.

Geneva shrugged. "Perhaps I didn't think that part through too clearly. I was under a lot of stress at the time, so sue me."

"Stop interrupting her," Drake scolded. "Go on."

"I didn't want him to find me, so I climbed up the mountain trail and hid behind a boulder. When he came back, he wasn't carrying any of his treasure, so I assumed he was looking for us. First, he headed to our car and saw you passed out in the back seat. He must not have considered you a threat, because he let you be."

"Wait, so you went to hide and left me in the car?" Drake asked.

Geneva shrugged again. "What was I going to do with you?

I couldn't carry you up the mountain by myself, and I guessed since you were already unconscious, he wouldn't mess with you."

"Stop interrupting her," Ingrid scolded. "We haven't heard any of this story." Ingrid grinned at Drake, and he smiled in return.

"Okay," Drake said. "You hid up the mountain, and?"

"And after Lorenzo found you, he started looking for me. He checked in and around both vehicles, and actually walked a few feet up the mountain path before he stopped. I thought for sure I'd get caught. Although he couldn't see me from the ground, he'd easily spot me if he came more than fifteen feet up the trail. Anyway, when he couldn't find me, he left to get the treasure. It must have been a lot, because he made two trips. The first time, he dumped several old leather bags into the bed of his pickup. That's when he made his mistake."

"What was that?" Drake asked.

"Before he put the bags in the truck, he leaned his gun against the back tire. When he left for the rest of the loot, he forgot to take it with him. When he disappeared down the hill, I ran down the trail, grabbed the shotgun and waited on the far side of our Fiat. When he came back, I threatened him with his own weapon."

Ingrid clapped. "That's incredible!"

"What happened next?" Drake asked.

"Next was mostly luck. As I stood there pointing a gun at Lorenzo, trying to decide what to do about him, an off-duty cop, who just happened to be out for a joyride on his new motorcycle, took an interest in us. Of course, he pulled his gun on me, and when he did, I dropped the one I had. It took about three minutes for me to tell him what happened, and when he looked in the pickup bed and saw the goods, he put Lorenzo in handcuffs. Then he radioed in for backup and told me to find Ingrid and Allie."

"We thought you were him coming back to finish us off," Ingrid admitted. "I almost wet myself. I was so scared."

"So, then they got an ambulance for me and drove me all the way back here?" Drake asked.

"Not at all," Allie said. "They brought in a helicopter for you. Landed it right in the middle of the road."

"It was a beautiful flight. The scenery was marvelous," Geneva said.

"You got to enjoy the ride, and I slept through the whole thing?" Drake asked.

Geneva laughed. "Don't worry. I took pictures."

Ingrid gathered all the playing cards and shoved them back into the box while Allie put on her coat.

"Where are you two going?" Drake asked.

Allie walked over to Drake's bedside, leaned over, and kissed him on the forehead. "Ingrid and I are going to help a friend with a project. Geneva will stay here to keep you company, and we'll be back later."

"Maybe," Ingrid said.

Allie nodded vigorously. "Right. If you're lucky, we'll be back later. Or we might go to the spa."

"You girls are such jerks," Drake said.

"That's why you love us," Allie said.

Allie and Ingrid left the room, leaving the couple to themselves.

*

Four days later, Allie parked the Fiat in an open spot right in front of Victoria's Leonardo da Vinci Museum. Before the four got out of the car, Victoria stood outside, waiting to welcome the group.

"Thank you for coming!" Victoria said as she greeted each person with cheek kisses and welcomed them into the museum.

"This is coming along nicely," Allie said as she stepped into the main room. All the exhibit cases had moved into the center of the room and sat covered with drop cloths. A fresh coat of paint covered all the walls, and murals representing Leonardo's drawings were penciled in over the fresh paint. "This will look fantastic when it's finished."

"Let's go sit," Victoria said. She led the group to the same small break room they'd occupied.

"When do the new exhibits open?" Allie asked.

Drake's attention perked up. "You're putting the things Lorenzo stole on display here?"

Victoria laughed. "Oh, no. Everything he found was fake."

"Fake?" I don't understand.

"Everything in those chests were reproductions," Allie said. "A few of the visitor bureaus around Northern Italy got the idea of doing a scavenger hunt of sorts based on the works of well-known Italian artists. Since the legend of the lost treasures of Leonardo da Vinci is so prevalent in this area, they thought it only natural to use that cave to 'hide' the Leonardo stuff."

"Are you saying we were chasing around the country for nothing? None of that was real?" Drake asked.

"Come with me," Victoria said.

Victoria led the group from the storeroom to a side room. The only things in the room were eight crates. The two largest were the size of an easy chair, the rest the average size of a piano bench.

"What's all this?" Drake asked.

"The lost works of Leonardo da Vinci," Victoria said.

"But where did you get it?"

Victoria pointed at Allie. "From her."

Drake passed Allie a look that she'd seen plenty of times before and knew she needed to offer an explanation.

"Let's go sit back down and I'll explain," Allie said.

Once everyone took their seats back in the breakroom, Allie began speaking.

"Two days after our encounter with Lorenzo, Ingrid and I drove back out to the valley."

"Why?" Drake asked.

"Because when Lorenzo had me search the cavern, I found this," Allie said, pulling out her phone. She opened her photos and showed everyone the picture of the intertwined knots embedded in the cave wall. "I figured since I'd already found the chests, I could withhold this little nugget from Lorenzo. I already knew the stuff in the trunk was fake."

"How?"

"The journal I picked up had the company's stamp on the back cover. Anyway, the symbol concealed the hiding spot of all those things that Victoria has in those crates. We contacted Victoria, and she took it from there."

Victoria waved her hand. "It was no effort on my part, I just hired movers."

"Won't there be some question of ownership?"

"Well, I have the good news and the bad news for you regarding that," Victoria said. "The bad news is, according to law, the state owns everything you found. The good news is, you will receive a splendid finder's fee based on the value of the items recovered. I suspect you will get more money than you've ever dreamed of."

"What happens to the artifacts?" Drake asked.

"That is the good news for me. Since I already have connections within the antiquities bureau, I've arranged to catalog the items and display many of them here. Of course, I don't have the room for everything, so I'll share with other museums in Milan, but the entire trove will stay in this region."

"That's good," Drake said. "I was, however, hoping to add something to my personal collection."

"You don't have a collection," Allie said.

Drake shrugged. "Just dreaming."

Victoria smiled. "Well, perhaps I can convince the government to let you hold on to a little something for us, just as a loan, of course."

"Of course."

"Now, would you like to see what you found?" Victoria asked.

Drake erupted in a wide grin. "How is that even a question?"

*

The next morning, after breakfast, the four walked along the lakeshore.

"Can you believe all that stuff?" Drake said. "Journals, art, inventions, sketches. It's going to take Victoria years to catalog all of those items."

"I can tell you she's looking forward to it. She can't wait to get started. It will be a boon to this region, and Italy in general," Ingrid said.

"So, with this all behind us, what do we do now?" Drake asked.

"We get back to vacationing like normal people," Geneva said. "With geocaching, and shopping, and taking pictures of all the things we encounter."

Drake stopped and looked out over the water. It was a perfect day. The sun glowed in the sky, causing a reflection of diamonds on the surface of the lake. The bright blue sky carried but a single lazy cloud.

"I wasn't thinking about vacation. I've been thinking more about the future, and the future I want to have is one with you." Drake removed an object from his pocket and dropped to a knee. "Geneva, I've loved you since the day we met. I can't picture a future without you. Will you marry me?"

Geneva stared into Drake's eyes for a moment, and then focused on the engagement ring he held between his fingers. Her eyes went from the ring, to Drake, to Ingrid, to Allie, and back to Drake.

"Of course, I'll marry you," Geneva said. "Get up here."

Drake stood and placed the ring on her finger. The couple

embraced and then kissed.

"That was sweet, wasn't it?" Allie asked.

"Sure was," Ingrid said.

"Did you get it all on video?"

"Every moment."

"It's about time he asked her. He's been walking around this entire trip with that ring in his pocket like an idiot," Allie said.

"I'm surprised it didn't end up at the bottom of the mountain," Ingrid said.

The couple broke their embrace, and Drake looked at his other two friends. "We can hear you."

Allie shrugged, then leaned in and gave Ingrid a quick kiss. "Let's leave the lovebirds alone for a while. Now that everything else is out of the way, can we finally go find some gelato?"

ABOUT THE AUTHOR

Dan DeKoning was born and raised in Milwaukee, Wisconsin, and currently lives in Knoxville, Tennessee with his wife and their cats.

He is a storyteller and poet who loves to write in a variety of genres and themes. He is also a voracious reader who loves to read anything he can get his hands on.

When he's not writing, you can find him hunting for treasures in used bookstores, or out exploring the planet, or geocaching, or searching for adventures and stories to tell.

# ALSO BY DAN DEKONING

This is Dan DeKoning's complete library at the time of publication, but Dan has new books coming out all the time. Sign up for his newsletter at DanDeKoning.com to stay up to date on new releases.

<u>Fiction</u>
*Déjà Vu*
*The Haunting of Hyacinth House*
*How Deep the Darkness*

<u>Geocaching Mystery Series</u>
*The Cacheland Conspiracy*
*The Quincy Bay Quandary*
*The Secret of the Seven Valleys*
*The Geocaching Mystery Omnibus – Volume 1*

<u>Codi Cassidy Cozy Mystery Series</u>
*Acoustics and Alibis*
*Ballads and Bloodshed*
*Codas and Calibers*
*Codi Cassidy Omnibus – Volume 1*

<u>Poetry Collections</u>
*Lost and Found*
*Random Thoughts*